THE MARINER'S SECRET

BY

MARY TOMASI-DUBOIS

PublishAmerica
Baltimore

First printing

All characters appearing in this work are fictitious. Any resemblance to real persons, living or dead, is purely coincidental.

ISBN: 1-4241-1178-1
PUBLISHED BY PUBLISHAMERICA, LLLP
www.publishamerica.com
Baltimore

Printed in the United States of America

To Paul,
whose inspiration, suggestions and help
made this work possible.

Enjoy!
Mary Tomasi-Dubois
'06

Prologue

Matt Townsend was a handsome nineteen-year-old. His intelligent expression, along with the experiences of the past seven years, gave him an air of sophistication of a man twice his age. He stood in the large library, his green eyes focusing intently on the painting, their gaze softened by the smile on his face.

Matt unconsciously ran a hand through his light brown hair as the room brought back a rush of memories and mixed emotions for him. The icy stare of the old mariner in the portrait no longer seemed as mysterious as it had the first time he saw the painting. "No, I know your secrets now, ol' Captain," Matt said; and his thoughts drifted to 1997, when he was twelve, and of all the things he and Heather had experienced in the old San Francisco house.

Chapter 1

Matt and Heather were smart enough, in spite of their young ages, to know that Roger Hill, their great aunt's butler and chauffer, was up to something. He was all smiles around Great-Aunt Estelle, but when it was just him and the children or when he thought it was just him and his wife Manar, their governess and maid, Roger Hill took on a totally different character.

Yeah, he was up to something all right, and it was no good.

Roger was a tall, lanky man with pasty skin that made him look as though he came right out of a crypt. In fact, that's how Matt and Heather came up with their nickname for him, "The Crypt Keeper."

"I don't see how she can kiss him," Matt said.

"Yeew," Heather answered, screwing up her face as though she had a nasty taste in her mouth. Even though, at eleven, Heather didn't yet think of any boy romantically, she couldn't imagine being married to someone like Roger Hill, ever. "And how can Manar let him put his arms around her? It'd give me the shivers. I'll bet his hands are cold as ice, they're so skinny and blue all the time."

"Well, he was nice enough when we first met him. I mean, remember how he'd take Manar and us to the zoo and buy us ice cream," Matt reminisced.

"I know. And remember how he was always trying to win stuffed animals at the carnival for us? Maybe that's why Manar fell in love with him in the first place. She's always saying 'Looks aren't everything. It's character and kindness that count.'"

"Yeah, he's a character all right, but what happened to the kindness?" Matt answered with a cynical tone in his voice.

"I know, huh? Manar is always making excuses for him whenever he's mean to her. I think she's been unhappy for a very long time," Heather mused.

"Well how could she be happy? He's mean to her all the time, except whenever Aunt Estelle is around."

"Yeah, it was better before The Crypt Keeper came to live here," Heather said. She wished Manar had never spoken to Roger Hill that day at the Japanese Friendship Garden in Golden Gate Park. But then, Manar had been lonely, Heather could tell.

Manar Jibari was born, raised, and well educated in Teheran, Iran. She came from a moderately wealthy merchant family and her life had been very similar to that of American children—that is, until the regime change and the overthrow of the Shaw.

It became more and more difficult to adjust to the lifestyle changes imposed on everyone. But even more difficult for Manar to bear was the death of her father. He had been killed as a suspected conspirator against the Iatollah, further shattering her life. Her mother just barely managed to escape to Turkey with Manar and her brother, Baruse—and from there, eventually to the United States. But, even though her life in America gave her some normalcy, Manar was never fully herself again and her demeanor took on a brooding quality.

Becoming Matt and Heather's governess was the highlight of Manar's early career. She had worked as a governess since she was eighteen, eventually landing a job with an English couple who had been temporarily transferred to the United States while working for a large computer firm. Once the couple's transfer was up, though, Manar had to look for employment with another family. She came highly recommended and had excellent credentials when she was introduced to Matt and Heather's parents, Jon and Josie Townsend. They liked her and hired her immediately. So, Manar had been the children's governess since they were toddlers.

The Townsends treated Manar as though she were a member of the family, beginning with the very first day. They were even the ones who had sponsored her and helped her become an American citizen. Manar went with the Townsends everywhere—on family gatherings, on vacations, on visits to other families—in fact, because her own mother had died two years earlier and she had completely lost track of her brother, she began to feel that the Townsends were her family and almost felt as though Matt and Heather were her own children. But, while she was proud to be making her way as a new American, she wished she didn't have to take care of other people's children but instead, had a home and family of her own.

Finally, Matt broke the silence along with Heather's daydreaming. "You mean it was better before *we* came to live here," he said sourly.

At almost thirteen, Matt was feeling the rigidity of his great-aunt's household closing in on him. He was eager for adventure, and he suspected his best friend, Heather, his sister was too. Matt often wondered what their lives would have been like if their parents hadn't been killed that fateful day in 1989, and if they didn't have to live in their aunt's stuffy old row house. Yes, it was beautiful and luxurious, and yes, the bay views were fantastic, but Matt wished for something more. He wished he could be living on a ranch in Texas or on an island in Washington State—or in Hawaii. Yeah, that'd be great! Swimming with dolphins and whales, fighting off sharks, looking for sea caves; and he'd never have to wear street clothes again, just swim trunks and flip-flops.

"Oh, it's not so bad here," Heather said, interrupting Matt's daydream this time. Heather's brown eyes sparkled with delight at the thought of her own bedroom all made up to look like that of a princess. As she sat there in her blue dress, with her golden hair pulled back, Matt had to admit to himself that she did look like Cinderella ready for the ball. But he wasn't going to let her pretty face deter him.

"You mean you'd rather live here with Aunt Estelle, than with Mom and Dad?" Matt said, and turned his back to Heather, obviously upset.

"No, I really do wish we were with Mommy and Daddy, but—I mean if we can't, then I'm glad we live here," Heather said with a shrug.

It had been a little over eight years since their parents' death, but Heather's relationship with them was frozen in 1989, when they were still alive and she was only three years old, and so she still thought of them as Mommy and Daddy. Many of her memories of them had faded. What she could still remember, though, was her mother's beautiful brown eyes looking deep into her own as she was sung to sleep with a lullaby. And she remembered her dad's smile as she ran towards him, wrapping her arms around his legs when he came home from the research lab.

"So," Heather continued talking, "I try not to think about it."

Chapter 2

The school year was almost over and the buzz around school was all about vacations—who was going where and with whom, what places would be visited, and what the means of transportation would be—airplane, car, train, or ship. Everyone was excited, everyone, that is, but Matt and Heather. Their vacation wouldn't be a vacation at all. They'd just go to the Exploratorium with Manar and The Crypt Keeper, or possibly on a picnic at Stinson Beach or Muir woods. Or worse yet, they'd be stuck in their great-aunt's row house, alone with Manar and The Crypt Keeper, while their aunt visited Europe. Then, when she'd return, because she'd feel guilty about having left them, she'd take them to lunch or dinner at one of her favorite stuffy ol' restaurants—yuck!

Matt *yearned* for something more. He would be thirteen in two weeks. His life had to change soon or he'd go mad! It was so boring living in the old house.

Matt's thoughts now drifted to the first day he saw the majestic row house perched on a rise in the wealthy Marina District of San Francisco. He and Heather had been driven to their new home directly from their parents' funeral. It was a gray and dreary day, reflecting their mood. They sat in silence in the big, black limousine. Remnants of the earthquake's devastation were still evident in parts of the neighborhood.

The driver had to take a circuitous route to avoid the police barricades set up to protect citizens from the potential collapse of structures. Parts of the area looked as though they were a war zone. Their great-aunt's house was one of the few that had remained untouched.

When they finally reached the home's front entrance, they were escorted to the front door by their aunt and the limousine driver, who had walked around and opened the door, holding an enormous black umbrella over their heads in an attempt to stave off the lightly falling drizzle. But he was so tall, the back of Matt's neck got wet anyway, causing him to shiver. As they slowly approached the house, the two large, leaded-glass doors mysteriously opened, revealing the foyer and grand staircase. Matt and Heather just stood there looking up in awe, and Matt shivered again, this time wondering what fate lay before them.

The two had spent the next few weeks exploring. The house's architecture provided a never-ending source of intrigue for them and they could always find something fun to do, from sliding down the winding banister to playing hide-and-seek in all the mysterious rooms and corners. The garden and potting shed held their own fascination as well.

But, today, on the cusp of becoming thirteen, Matt realized he had tired of all of the home's interesting nooks and crannies long ago. He remembered he had especially liked the servants' staircase that wound discreetly behind all the rooms from the kitchen up to the back hallway leading to the bedrooms, but that no longer held a fascination for him either. He had also enjoyed reading the thick book on the history of the house and of the unscrupulous mariner whose painting hung in a dark corner of the library, and who, it was rumored, had used indentured Chinese laborers to build the house—but, that, too, lacked appeal. Matt had, in fact, exhausted all avenues of pleasure once derived from his explorations of the old house.

Early on, Matt and Heather had agreed that the library was the neatest room in the whole house, and their next favorite besides their bedrooms. But, even its charms were beginning to wear thin, and it felt more like a prison to Matt than the cozy cocoon it had once been.

The walls and ceiling of the library were paneled in a rich American cherry wood, creating a cozy feeling in spite of the room's large scale. In the evenings, before bed, Matt and Heather liked to either sink into the overstuffed burgundy sofas and chairs to read, or lie on the floor to play games. The only nice thing about living with their great-aunt, in Matt's opinion, was the fact that she was constantly buying them books since reading was one of her favorite things to do too. She would always say, "There is very little else a child can do that is better than reading." So, she had had one of the bottom library shelves cleared of old ledgers to make room for new books for the children.

Aunt Estelle enjoyed retiring to the library along with Matt and Heather to sip her after-dinner coffee. She would muse about their interest in the room, and often said how funny it was that this should be their favorite room. "It was your Uncle Hubert's favorite room too. He picked all the furnishings and a lot of the books."

Whenever Aunt Estelle talked about Uncle Hubert, Matt could imagine the uncle he had never met sitting in one of the large leather chairs, smoking his favorite cigar, his hand around a cut-glass snifter of cognac, resting on the elaborately carved mahogany table next to him.

It was a man's room all right. There were trophies and models of ships and narrow-gauge trains everywhere. Matt had especially loved to listen to the Saint Michael's clock that sat atop the mantel, its chimes different from the ordinary Westminster chimes of every other clock he had heard. And on a cold rainy day, he and Heather loved to lie on the Persian carpet, listening to the crackling of the fire in the green-marbled fireplace with its carved mahogany surround and large, open hearth. They would quietly lie there, mesmerized by the eerie dancing shadows cast by the fire's glow, lost in their own thoughts.

On days when Roger had driven their aunt downtown to go shopping and Manar was busy doing laundry, Matt and Heather would head for the library to play the majestic old pipe organ that sat in the corner. They didn't believe their aunt's insistence that it didn't work properly and that she'd "have to get someone in to fix it one of these days." Everyone in the household seemed to ignore the fact that on some nights, the sound of organ music could distinctly be heard wafting upstairs from what seemed like the library—everyone but Matt and Heather that is.

Their favorite room held still another fascination for them—the sliding, library ladder. Its purpose was to reach the upper shelves of the twelve-foot-high bookcases that wrapped around three walls of the room. Instead, they'd take turns pushing one another on it until Manar would finally yell from the laundry room to "stop behaving like wild animals."

For Matt, the room had always inspired thoughts of sailing to faraway places and of adventure, and maybe that's why he couldn't derive as much pleasure from it these days, because *he* wasn't sailing to faraway places and he certainly wasn't having an adventure!

The only spot that still held some interest for him was his and Heather's secret spot in their favorite room. Their finding it was purely by accident. One day, the inspiration the old library evoked of a captain's quarters on an old sailing ship had induced Matt to bombard Heather with wadded-up note paper—and the battle began.

Matt had strategically placed himself behind one of the armchairs while Heather looked for a place to hide and plan her own moves. That's when she crawled on the floor and hid behind the sofa. It was a perfect spot. It was a narrow, tunnel-like space, created by the wall on one side, the sofa on the other, and the custom-made sofa table as its ceiling.

"Whoa," she said. "Look at this, Matt."

Matt dropped the wadded-up paper he held in his hand and crawled next to Heather. "Cool," he said. "What a cool hiding place." And they had been hiding there ever since, for almost six years now.

They even had a stash of candy bars, cookies, and other junk food their aunt otherwise refused them. Shortly after finding the spot, they had rummaged through the kitchen and found a small plastic storage tub in one of the cupboards. It fit perfectly under the back of the sofa, hiding their stash until they could get at it.

Somehow today, though, even that no longer held the same interest for Matt. Instead he lay on his bed, thinking of faraway lands, of what he might be when he grew up, of everything but his boring life in his Great-Aunt Estelle's house.

Chapter 3

The big day finally arrived, but Heather seemed more excited about it than Matt.

"What's wrong, Matt? Aren't you excited about being thirteen?" Heather asked.

"Yeah, I guess so."

"What's the matter, you've been mopey for two weeks now. Come on, you're going to have a party, cheer up."

"A party? You call what we have a party?" Heather knew to what Matt was alluding.

Other than when they were attending private school, Matt and Heather were seldom around other children. Aunt Estelle didn't like having what she called "little heathens" running around, destroying all her fine things, and seldom allowed young visitors to call on Matt and Heather. So, contrary to every other child of their age, not only did Matt and Heather find the summer months somewhat boring, but likewise, birthday parties and holidays too. These generally incorporated cocktails, quickly degenerating into dull, adult social gatherings rather than proper children's events. They were almost exclusively attended by adults, some of whom did occasionally bring a grandchild or niece or nephew to play with Matt and Heather. But that was rare since the visiting children had found the household boring too.

And so, on this occasion, Matt and Heather were the only partygoers below the age of eighteen. After a polite thank you to everyone, Matt and Heather excused themselves and escaped to the library rather than hang around and listen to silly adult chatter.

Heather fell onto the sofa, grabbing her latest edition of *Cricket* magazine on the way down. "Ahhh! So, what'll we do now, Matt?"

"Ugh, I wish we could escape from here," Matt said, trying to immerse himself in a computer game. But, it was no use, the game was boring. He had played it, for what to him, seemed like a million times.

Even though there was a television in addition to the computer in the library, Matt and Heather were restricted to only two hours per day of watching it, and then only on selected channels or programs. They were only allowed two hours on the computer too, originally just for research and homework, but then Aunt Estelle relented when Manar had given them a computer game for Christmas one year. So that was it. *One stupid computer game,* Matt thought and pounded the end button, walking away from the screen.

"OK. Come on. I'm gonna give you my special present now," Heather said, and headed for their secret hideaway behind the sofa. "Aren't you coming? Come on."

"Why do we have to go there for it? Why can't you give it to me here?"

"Because it's more special in our secret place."

When they finally settled in, Heather handed Matt his gift and he hurriedly ripped the wrapping paper from the present, guessing it was a book by the shape of it. But it wasn't just an ordinary book, it was a diary, similar to the log book their dad had used to jot down his sudden insights and creative solutions to problems.

"When I saw it at the stationery store, I suddenly remembered Daddy and how he was always writing things down," Heather said. "I know how you like to read and take notes, so I thought this would be perfect."

The children knew very little of their parents, just that they had been scientists conducting research. The truth is, their parents had been successful biochemists who, in 1988, had started a biotechnical firm, SafGen, in Burlingame, California. The firm was under contract to other larger companies to conduct genetic research. But Jon and Josie Townsend had been privately conducting their own research to find the genetic markers for intelligence. Once discovered, the markers could have a major impact on society—with a potential for good or bad. Consequently, when news leaked that they might have, in fact, been successful, their research raised some controversy over the fact that genetic manipulation to produce a race of super-intelligent babies would be available to only the wealthy; or worse, if the process were ever to get into the wrong hands, could be manipulated to produce a race of zombie-like humans, obeying the commands of a fiend.

"Thanks, Heath, the diary is perfect," Matt said and hugged her, forgetting for a moment how bored he had been earlier.

They both lay on the floor, head to head, talking of their drab lives when Matt, who was lying very close to the wall, suddenly discovered a feature that started at the baseboard and went up the paneled wall. It looked like an opening of about two square feet. Matt had never noticed it before. It was a chink in the paneling.

"Whoa. Look at this!" Matt said. And his heart began pounding in excitement and anticipation, hoping he had discovered a secret trapdoor to a passageway (possibly added by the Chinese laborers who built the house long ago).

Matt tried to pry the door open with his fingertips. "I just can't get a good enough grip to open it."

"Hold on, I'll get the letter opener." Heather backed out of the tunnel-like space and ran to the desk and grabbed the sterling-silver letter opener. "Here Matt," she said, and tossed it to him from the end of the sofa.

Matt stuck the blade end in on the right side, but couldn't get enough leverage to pry the door open. He slid the blade around the top and over to the left when they both heard a click and the panel opened, revealing a small passageway barely big enough for an adult.

Both their hearts began pounding this time. Matt poked his head through, but it was so dark he could hardly see what was beyond the threshold. He decided to venture further, prodding Heather to come with him.

"No. I'm scared. Anyway, shouldn't I stay here and make sure no one catches us?"

"Yeah, that's a good idea," Matt whispered as he maneuvered his body around to sit at the opening rather than have only his head poking through. He was sitting on what felt like a ledge with his feet dangling in air. As he scooted forward, to his surprise he began sliding down a forty-five-degree ramp.

"Whooooa!" Heather heard Matt's shout trail off into the abyss as she was left there kneeling at the opening. She listened for the sound of Matt's voice to assure her that everything was OK, but still on the alert for one of the adults, should they decide to see what the two children had been up to for so long.

Chapter 4

On this, his maiden voyage into the unknown, Matt entered a dim counterpart library. While it had many of the same features of the library he was so used to, it was somehow different. There were overstuffed mohair settees in dark colors, not the usual leather sofas and chairs Matt was used to. In the corner sat the majestic pipe organ. Above it the familiar painting of the old mariner still stood watch. But the paint seemed fresh and brighter, with none of the aged patina one would expect of an old painting. Matt walked closer to the pipe organ. It looked like the same one, but the wood was shiny and new and the labels on the pulls weren't worn like the ones he was familiar with.

A prickly feeling began to creep up on the back of Matt's neck and his stomach started getting queasy—it was time to find his way back to the real library and to Heather.

Matt frantically tried to climb the ramp, but his feet kept slipping back. He was beginning to feel faint. He sat on the floor at the base of the ramp, exasperated, trying to think of a solution and trying to calm himself. He looked around for something to help with his assent when he spotted a lever at the side of the ramp. Matt stood up, reaching for it with a quivering hand. He gingerly took hold of the lever and slowly pulled. There was a loud crack, then a creaking sound, and Matt jumped back in fright.

The ramp flipped over, revealing stairs.

Matt slowly tested the first step. He stood on it for a short while to make sure it would hold his weight and wouldn't suddenly flip back over, exposing the ramp side. When he was satisfied, he quickly climbed the rest of the steps, hoping to get to the top before the ramp did reappear.

Finally, he was at the top and through the opening. He took in a lungful of fresh air, realizing the air in the library he had just visited was dank and musty. Heather was still on her knees, staring and waiting for him to say something.

Breathlessly, Matt started to describe what he had just seen, when they both heard footsteps on the marbled floor beyond the library doors. It was The Crypt Keeper rapidly approaching. He would be through the door in a matter of seconds.

Chapter 5

Matt and Heather just barely managed to close the secret door, slide out from their hiding place, and sit on the sofa, Matt jotting down notes in his new log book, and Heather reading her magazine.

"It's upside down," Matt whispered, out of breath.

"What?" Heather asked, puzzled.

"Your magazine, it's upside down."

"Oh," and Heather just barely managed to get it right side up when The Crypt Keeper slowly opened the library doors.

The Crypt Keeper stared at the two of them, first Matt then Heather, causing shivers to go up and down her spine. His beady eyes looked like two small yellow spotlights glowing from beneath his one large bushy eyebrow. The rest of his face was in shadow as he stood in the doorway, one large silhouette, arms outstretched holding the doorknobs.

Finally his raspy voice broke the thick silence. "Madam wishes your presence in the drawing room." The Crypt Keeper stood there, waiting, as though he were a jailer about to take his prisoners to their doom.

Matt and Heather got up and slowly walked towards the tall skinny man. Matt stopped just in front of The Crypt Keeper, looking at him defiantly, waiting for him to move away from the doorway. The Crypt Keeper stared back.

Finally, he dropped one hand from the doorknob, allowing Matt to brush past. Matt's shoulder pushed The Crypt Keeper's arm aside and this time Matt looked straight ahead, trying not to reveal how much he detested the man. Heather followed, but unlike Matt, she couldn't stop looking up at The Crypt Keeper and turned sideways to scoot past him, trying not to touch any part of his body with hers.

No one knew very much about Roger Hill's past. When Manar had told Estelle Furgeson she had received a proposal of marriage, Mrs. Furgeson insisted she meet this man. "My dear," she had said to Manar, "as your employer, I feel responsible for your happiness and your future. So, I would like to meet your gentleman friend. After all, I am much older than you and I think I have enough experience to tell if he would be right for you."

Matt remembered the day Roger Hill first came to the old house. He disliked the man from the start. He seemed disingenuous with his overly polite behavior. Roger explained that he had been unemployed for a short while, but said that he knew a lot about cars and had driven for a limousine company, taking passengers to the airport or out on special occasions. He said that currently, though, he was employed as a night guard, but was rather unhappy with that since he wasn't using his talents nor intelligence to their fullest potential. He never mentioned his employment with SafGen.

Mrs. Furgeson was completely enamored with Roger, and because she needed one anyway, she decided to offer him a job as her chauffer and butler, but not until after his and Manar's wedding. That way, he could move into Manar's room and the problem of housing another employee would be solved. Roger accepted. His plan for gaining unlimited access to the old house had worked.

The wedding was held in the drawing room of Aunt Estelle's large home. The only people in attendance were Aunt Estelle and a few of her friends who had a special fondness for

Manar because of her caring treatment of their grandchildren or nieces and nephews whenever they were brought to play with Matt and Heather. There were no guests in attendance who knew Roger. Matt was the ring bearer and Heather was the flower girl. Manar cried, wishing her real family could've been there to share in her happiness.

So, Roger Hill had been the family butler and chauffer for three years, and Aunt Estelle had remained completely satisfied. It was only Matt and Heather who suspected The Crypt Keeper of no good, even though neither they nor anyone else knew of his secret past and how much of a threat to their safety he really was.

Unbeknownst to them, Roger had been originally employed as head of security for SafGen. However, he had been quietly dismissed on the night of October 16, 1989, when Jon Townsend had found Roger taking snapshots of the log book for the genetic research he and Josie had compiled. The log explained their process for identifying the biomarker for intelligence.

When Jon walked into his private office and found Roger bending over his desk, he confiscated the camera and asked Roger to leave the premises immediately. "I'll be filing charges this Friday, the eighteenth—be forewarned."

Roger, The Crypt Keeper, really wasn't on Matt's mind today, though. In fact, all the depressing feelings and thoughts he had had these past few weeks were completely gone. He was thinking of other more exciting matters now, and as he and Heather walked towards the drawing room, Matt whispered, "Wait 'til I tell you what I saw down there!"

Because of his long stilt-like legs, The Crypt Keeper was able to reach the drawing room doors first and slide them open, announcing Matt and Heather's arrival. "Master Mathew and Miss Heather, madam."

"Oh, come in, children. Mathew, your guests are about to

leave. Thank them for coming and for your gifts. Wasn't it nice of them to have been so generous?" Aunt Estelle said in a dramatic, slightly tipsy voice.

Why do I have to say all that, Matt thought, *didn't you just say it for me? And, besides, I'm not some little child that has to be told what's proper to say.*

"Achem," Matt cleared his throat. "Thank you all for helping me celebrate my birthday." Then he stood before each guest and shook their hands. "Thank you, Mr. Bartley, I needed a new baseball mitt. Thank you, Mr. and Mrs. Gannon, the sweater and slacks will be perfect for a visit to the De Young. Mrs. Hopland, I'm sure I'll enjoy the book on dinosaurs." And he continued on, amid whispers of what a polite young man he was and how proud Mrs. Furgeson must be. Finally, he had personally thanked everyone, including his Great-Aunt Estelle, who because of too much champagne, was unusually demonstrative and grabbed him in a bearish hug.

"Oh, my poor children," she said, and grabbed Heather too and held them both in her arms in a tight squeeze.

Aunt Estelle loved drama and loved to be the center of attention. She had never had children of her own, so by the time Matt and Heather became her wards she hadn't a clue as to how to deal with them. And so it seemed only natural to have Manar continue on as their governess—never mind that she had given her other responsibilities too. "Dear," she would say in her affected, sweet tone, "Won't you wash these few things for me? You haven't anything to do while the children are napping, have you? It would be such a help. Thank you." Or "Dear, would you mind terribly fixing me a little something to eat, and fix yourself something too. Thank you, dear, you're so kind." So, before long, Manar found her responsibilities went beyond just watching Matt and Heather; she really was a full-blown housekeeper too. If

Manar hadn't have loved the children so much, she might have considered finding work elsewhere.

Hubert Furgeson, Aunt Estelle's husband, had been in the diplomatic service and had traveled extensively throughout the world. His tragic death in 1979 on Flight 007 to Korea came as a severe shock to her. But, with a strong will and determination, within a short while Aunt Estelle was her old self again, throwing and attending parties.

Because of a successful career as a concert pianist, with everyone ooing and awing at her brilliant talent, Aunt Estelle had already built up a tidy sum in her bank account before marrying Mr. Furgeson. But his death had left her one of the wealthiest women in San Francisco, and now she enjoyed her life as a socialite, courted by politicians and foundations alike for her generous donations and influential support.

As a child prodigy, Estelle Furgeson had a demanding schedule of private piano lessons; constant practicing, recitals, and tours; and found herself surrounded only by adults. Consequently, coupled with the fact that she had no children of her own, she was uncomfortable around Matt and Heather and distant and stiff with them. The three of them did, at times, have quiet dinners together, though, but there was generally no laughter, only polite conversation, with a sprinkling of prodding by Mrs. Furgeson to "remember your manners."

Great-Aunt Estelle's idea of a good time for children was to take Matt and Heather to the symphony or the ballet. And, when she found the subject matter intelligent, she occasionally took them to see a children's play. Fortunately, neither Matt nor Heather knew their aunt also had plans to introduce them to the opera when they "were of appropriate age." If he had known, Matt certainly would have gone crazy with the prospect of his stuffy, ol' life only getting worse.

Chapter 6

Matt and Heather waited anxiously for the right time to head to their secret spot—and the hidden door. While they both had a slight aversion to its secrets, they were also drawn to uncovering its mysteries.

Even though Heather found Matt's tale of the strange, alternate library hard to believe, she had had dreams of falling and of dungeons and darkness. Actually, neither of them had been able to get a restful night's sleep, but, like all adventurous discoverers, they were compelled to continue on.

At breakfast Manar asked them what all the whispering was about, and The Crypt Keeper, who was sitting at the end of the kitchen table, polishing silver, looked suspiciously at them through his one bushy eyebrow. "Nothing," Matt said nervously, "I—I was just asking Heather if she wanted to play the computer game." They needed any excuse to get alone and devise their plan.

"No, you play the game," Heather said in an unusually high, stilted voice. "I'm going to finish reading my magazine."

The children finished their breakfast and uncharacteristically brought their dishes to the sink, looking steadily at Manar with an occasional glance at The Crypt Keeper. Manar knew from their behavior that something was up, but The Crypt Keeper didn't pay any further attention and wrote their actions off as insignificant childhood folly.

Matt and Heather finally reached the library. "We need enough time when we're sure that no one will be around to bother us," Matt said.

"Isn't Aunt Estelle going on that house tour with her woman's group Friday?" Heather said. "She'll be gone almost all day."

"Yeah, and Manar will be busy cleaning house and The Crypt Keeper will be washing and polishing the cars. That's perfect; we'll have practically the whole day alone." Matt could hardly wait.

Chapter 7

Friday finally arrived. The house was empty except for Matt and Heather, and Manar, who was busy upstairs tending to the bedrooms.

This time Matt didn't prod Heather into going with him through the secret door. "Stand watch again, Heather, and if you hear anything, start singing *Take Me Out to the Ball Game*, nice and loud."

"OK, be careful!"

"I will. Just make sure you keep listening for footsteps at the door."

Matt took the silver letter opener and his log book and crawled through to their spot behind the sofa. Heather followed. Matt slipped the blade of the letter opener in, and again, there was a click and the panel door opened.

Because of the novelty of the hidden door and because of their excitement of finding it the first time, neither had noticed the mariner's clock that hung on the left-side panel just inside the opening of the secret passageway. It must have been the way the sun's rays shone through the room at this early hour that caused Matt to look at it. "Whooa. What's this?"

Heather moved in to get a closer look. "What kind of clock is that?" Instead of the normal twelve hours she was used to seeing, this clock had more numbers. And where the 12 should have been, there was the number 24, right next to the digits 0,0. Puzzling over the strange clock, she noticed something even stranger. Heather silently pointed to the riddle inscribed in the paneling just below the clock. It read:

Tic Toc,
Tic Toc,
Time is in the hands of this clock.
Whether to go forward or whether to go back,
Whichever you choose will determine your track.
Never tarry longer then when the next watch is struck,
Or wherever you are,
That is where you are sure to be stuck!

After several moments of silence, Matt said, "I think I have an idea of where we might find out what this all means." He scooted out of their secret spot and walked to the bookshelves. "It's here somewhere." He was looking for the large book on the history of the old house to see if there was any information he might have overlooked mentioning the hidden door and strange clock. He flipped through the pages twice, but slapped the book shut with a sigh when he found nothing. Then he and Heather both began scanning the shelves looking for titles that might lead them in the right direction. They found several that seemed promising, but disappointingly, led nowhere.

Finally, Heather spotted one on the very top shelf that had the word "maritime" in it. *Hmmm,* she thought, *MariTIME, I wonder if that would have anything to do with it.*

She rolled the ladder to the shelf she needed to reach. Matt watched as she slowly climbed it. When she got to the top, she called down, "It's called *Maritime Rules of the Seas.* Do you think it would help?"

"Maybe. Bring it down. Let's look." Matt was willing to try anything at this point.

It was a thick book, and Heather held it close to her chest with one hand and held the side of the ladder with the other. She carefully stepped on each rung—first with one foot then the other, to make sure she wouldn't slip.

Matt watched her anxiously—it seemed to take her forever.

At last her feet touched the floor. Matt took the book from Heather's aching arm and laid it on the leather sofa. They both knelt in front of it, Heather watching as Matt slowly turned to the index to look up the words "clock" or "time." Under the heading Time, they found the sub-entry: Ship's Clock, page 329.

"I'll bet that has something to do with it," Matt said. "This house was built by a sea captain." He hurriedly flipped through the pages—350, 338—finally, page 329. Staring up at them was a diagram of a clock that looked exactly like the clock hanging inside the secret passageway. They both silently read the text.

DEVELOPMENT OF THE SHIP'S CLOCK

When a ship is underway at sea, it is necessary to man the essential operating stations, such as the navigation bridge and engine room, 24 hours a day. To accomplish this, the ship's crew is divided into "watches" which rotate duty time or being "on watch" in shifts usually four hours long.

In the sailing-ship era, before the development of mechanical clocks, the passage of each 4-hour watch was marked with an hourglass which ran 30 minutes each side. When the glass was turned over each half hour, the ship's bell was struck. Over time, a traditional pattern of striking the bell in couplets or pairs of strikes developed, which added a strike each half hour, thus, using an example of a watch beginning at noon:

Noon 8 bells (a new watch comes on duty)

12:30 1 bell

1:00   2 bells

1:30   3 bells

2:00   4 bells

2:30   5 bells

3:00   6 bells

3:30   7 bells

4:00   8 bells (the watchstanders are relieved by the next watch)

4:30   1 bell (and the pattern starts over)

A person standing watch could tell by listening to the bells where he was in his watch and how long it would be before the next watch came on deck. Also, if the strike was an even number, it was on the hour. If it was an odd number, it indicated it was the half hour, and which half hour it was. As mechanical clocks were developed, this bell pattern was transferred into ship's bell clocks, hence the 24 hours marked on the face.

They both finished reading at the same time and silently looked at one another. "Well," Matt finally said, breaking the silence, "that explains the clock. But what the heck does the riddle mean?"

Chapter 8

Heather began repeating the verse to herself, her gaze focused on some inner landscape while she tried to decipher its code.

In exasperation Matt said, "You can stay here and try to figure out the riddle, I'm going down the passageway again. Just remember to sing loud enough for me to hear if someone comes."

Matt scooted close to the edge of the opening—this time he was fully prepared to slide down the ramp. He found himself enjoying the ride and imagined it might be something like a ride at a theme park, even though he had never been on one.

Matt reached the bottom and got up, straightening his pants and shirt while he looked around. It was the same library he had visited the first time. He decided to venture further this time though. He slowly approached the double doors. In *his* home there would be a powder room to the right, just outside the library doors. He slowly opened the doors and poked his head around to the right. It appeared there was a powder room in this strange house too. He opened its door and felt around for the light switch, but instead of the familiar switch, he felt two buttons. He pushed the extended one in, and a bare light bulb suspended from the ceiling came on.

Matt stepped into the room. There weren't the modern

bathroom fixtures he was used to. Instead, a pedestal sink stood where the cabinet-mounted sink should be, and a wooden box stood where the toilet should be. A smaller, wall-mounted box hung above that, and a long chain with a wooden handle dangled from the overhead box. *Strange contraption; I'll have to remember to make note of it in my log,* Matt thought, and turned to exit while pushing the other button to turn off the glaring light bulb.

Matt tiptoed slowly down the hall with one hand skimming the wall; he wanted it there as support if he should come upon something that might startle him and cause him to lose balance.

He finally reached a door he guessed led to the kitchen. He opened the door and stopped mid-swing when its hinges began squeaking. Matt held his breath, squeezing the doorknob. He stood there not daring to make another move or sound, expecting to hear someone come running at him, shouting in protest at the intruder.

After what seemed like the longest minute, Matt exhaled and began breathing normally. He slowly opened the door all the way and a kitchen lay before him, but not the kitchen he was used to.

Matt looked across the white-tiled room to the windows overlooking Marina Boulevard. His eyes opened wide and he stood there, transfixed. This was the strangest sight he had seen so far in this strange version of his house.

There, before his very eyes, were horse-drawn carriages, Model-T Fords, and two steamships in the bay.

Matt turned around slowly, his eyes still wide open. He slowly walked through the doorway he had just entered. He didn't bother to close the door. When he made it to the hallway, he broke into a sprint, desperate to reach the library and the waiting ramp.

Breathless, he pulled the lever next to the ramp. There was the familiar crack and creaking, and the ramp obediently turned over to reveal its steps. Matt was already on the first step before the system had even completely settled into place. Skipping to every third step, Matt reached the top and flung himself into the kneeling Heather, both of them falling into a heap.

"What are you trying to do, Matt, kill us both?"

"Heather, you—you *have* to come with me. Even if it's just to prove I'm not going crazy!"

"What're you talking about? You look awful! What just happened down there?"

"Heath—I—I just saw old things. But they weren't old, they were new, but they're old things, ya know?" Matt couldn't find the right words to describe what he had just seen.

"No, I don't know. What did you see? Tell me, slowly."

"OK, OK. I—I saw carriages with horses," Matt started slowly. "And old cars, I think they're called Model-T's or something, and I saw a steamship. No, I mean two steamships. Like in the olden days, you know?" He was talking faster again.

"What do you mean steamships? How do you know they were steamships? And, anyway, people still drive old cars. It's a hobby. And the carriage was probably from Pier 39—you know they have that for the tourists." Heather was trying to convince herself as much as Matt. Somehow she suspected he had actually seen what he had described. And, if he had, she wasn't sure that would be a good thing.

They both knelt there in silence. Matt ran his fingers through his hair and shook his head. "What the heck *is* all this? The riddle. It says something about *'Time is on this clock—'*"

"No, it says *'Time is in the hands of this clock.'* Do you think that has something to do with all this?" Heather asked.

"Yeah, it must. Why would they've put a clock here at the opening? And why is there a secret opening in the first place?

Chapter 9

"What else does the riddle say?" Matt asked, as he scooted himself around to get a better look at it. *"'Whether to go forward or whether to go back, whichever you choose will determine your track'*? What the heck does that mean?"

"Sounds like time travel to me," Heather said. "Remember the movie *Back to the Future*? The scientist built a car that took the driver back and forth in time, just by setting the clock— Oh my gosh! Do you think that's what this does?" Heather's heart started pounding and she could feel her pulse in her throat.

Matt hadn't really heard Heather. He had guessed he was time traveling when he entered the library at the bottom of the ramp the second time. *"'Whether to go forward or whether to go back—*Hmm, I wonder what would happen if I changed the time," Matt whispered, just loud enough for Heather to hear, but not really speaking to her.

Matt took hold of the clock with both hands and carefully removed it from the hook. The clock was stopped at 10:00 a.m. "What time is it now?" he asked Heather.

"I don't know," she answered as she scooted out of their secret place. "Let me go look at the mantel clock. Oh, my gosh. It's already 11:30!" The time had rushed by, and two and a half hours had seemed like only one.

"Let me just set the time and wind —" Matt had just set the clock to 11:30 when he and Heather heard Manar call from the kitchen, "Hey, you two, lunch."

"Hurry up, Matt," Heather said, just loud enough for Matt to hear as she stood in front of the fireplace. "The Crypt Keeper will be coming to get us for lunch. Hurry."

Matt tried to hang the clock back up but couldn't get the slot lined up with the hook. His hands started shaking and he almost dropped the clock through the opening and down the ramp. He took a deep breath and angled his head so he could see the hook and hopefully successfully guide the clock's slot over it. He raised the clock slightly and slid it down over the hook, hoping to engage it, but missed again. He took another deep breath and blew it out through pursed lips. He raised the clock for the third time and slowly slid it over the hook again. This time it took hold, and not too soon. Those footsteps were unmistakable. Matt heard The Crypt Keeper's cursing under his breath at how he wasn't "a baby-sitter and if they missed lunch it would serve them right."

Matt closed the passageway door and hurriedly scooted out of the secret place, grabbing Heather's arm on the way out of the library. "Lunch, did I hear Manar call for lunch? Gosh, it's about time, I'm starved!" Matt said as he rushed past The Crypt Keeper with Heather in tow.

Matt hurried through his toasted cheese sandwich and gulped down his milk, passing up the oatmeal/raisin cookies. "Come on, Heather, I want to challenge you to a game of chess," he said as he glanced sideways at Manar and The Crypt Keeper to see if they were suspicious.

Heather was playing with the long strings of melted cheese between the two halves of her sandwich, and lazily swinging her feet back and forth in her chair. She had barely finished half the sandwich.

"Come on, Heather, bring the rest with you." Matt was getting impatient.

"No you don't!" Manar said. "Your aunt would kill all of us if she thought you were eating in there."

"But we sometimes have dessert in there," Heather said through a mouthful, staring at the cheese string dangling from the end of her sandwich and over her clutched fist.

"That's only when Madam asks for it. No. You finish eating here, and then you can go play your game," Manar said, not just because Estelle Furgeson wanted it that way but because she didn't want to have to clean up a mess in the library. No, the kitchen table was enough to clean.

Finally, Heather had finished her last cookie and second glass of milk as an exasperated Matt sat watching, his head supported in his hands with his elbows resting on the table.

The Crypt Keeper said he was going to the parts store to buy new wiper blades for the cars. But, even though Manar asked sweetly, he refused to go out of his way to buy air freshener. "Burn some of those scented candles. You should've remembered to add air freshener to your list for shopping day," he added sternly as he walked out the door to the garage.

Good. We won't be bothered the rest of the afternoon, Matt thought. He talked to himself as he and Heather walked back to the library. "Let's see. If it's almost one o'clock I would need to set the Mariner's clock to 1,300 hours, that'd be one o'clock in the afternoon, right? Yeah, twelve o'clock is twelve noon so 1,300 is one o'clock."

"Hmm-hmm," Heather answered, even though she knew he wasn't really talking to her.

After setting and winding the clock, Matt decided to go back down the passageway again, but this time he wanted Heather to go with him.

"No. I'm scared."

"But I'm telling you there's no one there and nothing to be scared of," Matt insisted.

Heather was finally convinced. "OK," Matt said. "I'll go

down first, and when I shout up to you, come down and I'll be right there at the bottom of the slide waiting."

Heather watched to see exactly what Matt did; she didn't want to make a mistake and fall off the ramp or something. Matt scooted to the edge of the opening and pushed himself off with his hands. Heather heard him giggle as he went sliding down.

Heather positioned herself exactly as Matt had done and said, "Here I come. Ready?"

Matt shouted back, "Yeah, come on."

Heather pushed herself off as she had seen Matt do. Sliding down the ramp made her feel giddy and she began giggling too. In no time, she was surprised to find herself sitting on what felt like damp sand at the base of the ramp. But that wasn't what surprised her. Instead of landing hard on her bottom the way she had on the slides at the children's park, this slide went all the way to the floor, or ground, or whatever it was.

Matt looked around, astonished. "What the—?"

"What's going on, Matt?" Heather asked, as she stood up brushing sand from her skirt.

They weren't in a library—not the one in their own home, nor the one Matt had described having visited. They were outside standing in the middle of a sandy marsh! The February sky was overcast and somber, with a cloud covering so thick it blocked out the sun, making it almost as dark as night.

"How can this be?" Matt wondered out loud. "What happened to the library?"

"I don't know, but it's scary here. Maybe you changed something by changing the clock, Matt. Didn't we agree it's probably a time-travel machine?"

"That's it! What time was it before I changed the clock?" he asked himself, trying to calculate what date it must be in the marsh.

"Let's see," Matt started on a long discussion with himself. "The clock read 10:00 when I saw carriages, old cars, and steamships—so, it was probably right around the turn of the century. So, if I moved the hands to 1,300 hours, that'd be— But wait a minute; I went all the way around the clock, counterclockwise instead of the short way. So, I must have traveled back in time to before the house was built. That's it, Heath! The clock *is* for time travel! That book I read about the history of the house? It explained that the house was built on landfill and that there had been a large marsh all along the old shoreline. Most of it was filled in and a small harbor was created."

"Please, Matt. Let's not stay. This is even creepier than I thought it would be. You can figure it all out back home. Let's just go, now!"

"Yeah, you're right. Anyway, I wanted you to see the old house. The way it was right after the captain had built it, not a marsh."

Heather turned towards the ramp. It was an eerie sight. The ramp seemed to appear from nowhere. "How are we going to get back up?"

"Stand back," Matt said, and pulled the lever. There was the loud cracking sound Matt was familiar with, but it caught Heather off guard, causing her to squeal at the sudden loud noise.

When they got safely back to their familiar spot, Heather said she was going to get another glass of milk from the kitchen and read her magazine. "I'm tired of clocks and riddles and secret passageways. I just want to lie down on that comfy sofa and veg out."

"OK," Matt said as he knelt before the clock. He wasn't ready to relax. This was significant. This had to be figured out.

Upon closer examination, Matt discovered that the clock was slightly different than the picture of the clock displayed in the maritime book. Evidently, the old captain had had a special mechanism added that allowed one to set the date as well as the time.

Six small knobs controlled digits corresponding to the date—one for the month, one for the day, and four for each digit of the year. "So," Matt pondered, "when I was fiddling with the clock, trying to set it to the current time, I somehow must have adjusted the yearly knobs back to a time before the house was built."

Matt looked at the date, sure enough it read [02][14][1][8][6][5]—February 14, 1865.

He quickly found the appropriate knobs and turned the year to 1917, a year after the house was believed to have been built. He left the month and day alone. "Now, let's go back down there and see what we have." Matt had to prove his theory was right. He had inherited a scientific mind from his parents and knew that theories must be tested out to be proven.

By this time Heather had returned to the library with her glass of milk and had already settled onto the sofa to read.

"I'm going back down, Heather. But before I go I want you to do something that will either prove our theory that the clock *is* a time-travel machine or disprove it once and for all."

"How can we possibly do that?" Heather wondered.

"I want you to write down instructions, seal them in an envelope, and hand them to me. I'll go down through the passageway, open the envelope and follow the instructions. When I return, we'll both check to see if I've followed them, proving that I've traveled back in time. So, come up with something we can check."

"OK, turn around. I don't want you to see what I'm writing." Heather tiptoed to the organ so that Matt wouldn't guess what she was up to. She knelt on the floor to check the lower, middle pedal. When she was satisfied, she slipped a stick of gum into an envelope along with a note and quickly sealed it. "Here, it's ready. Now, don't open it till you're down there. And hurry, it's getting late. Manar's almost finished with the cleaning and The Crypt Keeper will be coming home soon."

"Don't worry, I won't look, and I'll hurry. I want to prove this to myself too, ya know. And I don't want to get caught doing it!"

Matt descended into the darkness again. As he stood up at the base of the ramp, he was, in fact, back in the library of 1917. It worked! But he had to follow the instructions to prove it. Quickly he opened the envelope to read Heather's note. It read: *Chew this gum, then stick it under the lower, middle pedal of the organ.* "Good," Matt said. "Smart girl." Matt hurriedly chewed the gum until all the sweetness was gone. He stuck the moist wad under the pedal as instructed, and turned to pull the lever and ascend the stairs.

"OK," he said, emerging from the passageway and into the library where Heather was still lying on the sofa. "Let's go check the pedal."

Heather got goose bumps when she felt the hardened gum-wad where none had been when she had first checked. She dropped her hand and knelt there, transfixed. Matt knew by her expression that she had found the hardened gum, but he had to check too, as any true scientist would.

Neither one had heard the garage door open and close, signaling The Crypt Keeper's return home. Nor had they heard Manar walk into the library to retrieve Heather's empty milk glass. Fortunately, the passageway door was closed and Matt and Heather weren't behind the sofa in their secret spot but kneeling beneath the organ, strange as that was.

Chapter 10

It had been several weeks before Matt and Heather were able to get back to the secret passageway. The household was bustling to get everything ready for Aunt Estelle's annual European trip. Normally, this would have intrigued Matt and Heather with fantasies of going to exotic places, but now they had their own adventure. They just needed enough private time to explore the possibilities.

The day for Aunt Estelle's departure had finally arrived. Everyone piled into the black Lincoln Town Car; The Crypt Keeper at the wheel, Manar beside him, Aunt Estelle in the back behind Manar, and Matt behind The Crypt Keeper. That left Heather to sit on the hump in the middle, but she didn't mind. It provided her with the perfect vantage point to see the sights going by.

The children had fun going through the security arch at the terminal. Heather had forgotten to put her purse on the rolling ramp to be checked by the x-ray machine, and the coins inside caused the security buzzer to go off. So she had to back up, put her purse on the ramp and walk through the arch again. Aunt Estelle was, of course, annoyed at the delay. Even though there was plenty of time, she wanted to get her boarding pass, have a cup of coffee, and find good seating away from the rest of the crowd at the boarding gate.

The Crypt Keeper set Aunt Estelle's carry-on bag down near a group of seats in a remote alcove. Estelle Furgeson sat down with a great sigh. "Roger, get me a good cup of coffee, won't you? And bring the children some milk. Manar dear, you'd better go along and help. I'll sit here with the children and find out what they'd like me to bring them from my trip."

"Yes, ma'am," they both said in unison.

Matt and Heather sat for a while with their aunt, but the displayed items at the nearby gift shop fascinated them more. So, they were off wandering through the store and Aunt Estelle wasn't about to go after them.

Manar and Roger returned with the refreshments and Mrs. Furgeson had just enough time to finish her coffee when the flight attendant announced over her microphone, "First-class passengers boarding now, please."

Manar picked up the carry-on bag and The Crypt Keeper securely held Mrs. Furgeson's elbow, helping her out of her seat.

"Goodbye, children," Aunt Estelle said. "Come give your aunt a farewell kiss. Have a good summer and I'll have something special for you when I return."

The children pressed their noses to the large plate-glass window overlooking the runway. They wanted to stay until the plane Aunt Estelle boarded was out of sight, in spite of The Crypt Keeper's protests. He was showing his true colors in public now that Mrs. Furgeson was no longer present. "Oh, let the children stay and see the plane off," Manar said sweetly.

"What good will it do? She can't see them. Anyway, she's probably enjoying a glass of champagne right now and we have to watch these brats." Manar didn't answer. She didn't want to start a scene right there in the terminal.

Just then the plane started to taxi down the runway. It built up speed and, in spite of its heavy weight, lifted off. Like a giant silver bird, it tucked its wheels under its belly and flew higher until it was out of sight, disappearing into the pale blue sky.

The drive back home was silent, except for Matt and Heather's giggles. The Crypt Keeper's mood was obviously bitter. Manar remained silent the whole time. Matt and Heather sat in the back seat and kept making mocking faces of The Crypt Keeper at one another, causing the snickering. The Crypt Keeper looked ominously at them through the rearview mirror, but that just made them giggle more.

As they pulled into the short driveway and into the garage, Manar cleared her throat and said, "Do you think we could go out for a movie and some pie and coffee if I can get Azita to mind the children this evening?" And in a meek voice she added, "It would be nice to have an evening to ourselves, and the children enjoy Azita."

"I've got some things to do," The Crypt Keeper answered gruffly. "You go if you want to, but I'd skip the pie if I were you. You're putting on weight and it's not very attractive."

This comment made Manar uncomfortable, and she unconsciously smoothed her dress over her body in an effort to slim her contours.

Matt and Heather frowned at The Crypt Keeper. His comment had been uncalled-for. Manar looked beautiful to them, just as she was.

"No, I don't like going out alone," Manar said. "That's OK. The children and I will watch TV. I'm sure Madam wouldn't mind, especially if I select something appropriate for them to watch," she added with obvious disappointment in her voice.

The children were excited by the idea of an evening in front of the TV. Even though they were disappointed for Manar too, they liked the idea of curling up on the sofa with her, all wrapped up in the velvet throw.

"Can we have popcorn?" Heather asked.

"Yeah, and how about sodas?" Matt added. "I don't think Aunt Estelle would mind this time."

Manar smiled at the children then spoke to her husband in a vain attempt to create some semblance of harmony and romance in their lives. "Will you join us, Roger? When you've finished with your tasks?"

"You couldn't tie me down with those brats to watch some foolish television show! No. And besides, I've got too many important things to do than spend my time idly sitting around."

Manar's heart sank. Not so much at what Roger had just said or how he had said it, but because deep down she knew their relationship wasn't a relationship at all. She knew there was little love left in his heart for her—no matter how much she tried to foster it. She wasn't sure why he even stayed around. He didn't like the children and made it quite obvious. He just tolerated Madam Furgeson, in spite of his overly polite behavior whenever he dealt with her. And, it was more and more obvious that he didn't love Manar. So what was it that made him stay?

Chapter 11

Manar silently took off her coat and placed it on the hook behind the kitchen door. She put on her apron and busied herself making omelets and a green salad for dinner.

"Children, will you set the table, please?" she asked in a low voice. Matt and Heather could see her eyes glistening with sad tears. Without a word they placed a setting on each side of the kitchen table, giving one another knowledgeable glances as they did, communicating without saying a word.

The four of them sat down to eat. Suddenly, the thick silence was broken when The Crypt Keeper pushed his plate aside and said in a brusque voice, "Man can't get a decent meal nowadays," obviously upset at just having an omelet and salad.

"Would you like me to fix you something else?" Manar said, fighting back a full flood of tears.

"No. Appetite's gone now," The Crypt Keeper answered, and stood up so abruptly his chair fell back in a loud crash.

Everyone sat frozen. Manar hung her head and wept silently. Heather was about to cry too. Matt wanted to say something in Manar's defense but couldn't gather the right words. Instead, he just sat there staring at The Crypt Keeper, hatred oozing from him.

"What's your problem, little man?" The Crypt Keeper said.

Matt couldn't restrain himself any longer. "Why are you such a jerk?" he yelled defiantly.

The Crypt Keeper raised his hand, about to strike Matt when Manar shouted "NO!" and jumped up just in time to receive The Crypt Keeper's full blow. Manar fell to the floor, landing against the refrigerator. Her weeping was a full sob now and she held the red imprint of The Crypt Keeper's hand on her face.

Heather sat stunned, matching Manar's sobs with her own. Matt knelt next to Manar trying to soothe her, but glaring at The Crypt Keeper the whole time. The Crypt Keeper gave a gruff "ahhhgg" and made a backhand gesture in midair as if to suggest *I'm done with the lot of you*—and walked off.

"Come on, Heather, clean up the table," Matt said in a quiet but commanding voice. "Come on, Manar. It's all right. We'll clean up. Go sit in the library and find a movie we can watch. Heather and I'll pop some corn in the microwave and we'll have a good time."

"OK," Manar said, but she would rather have run a thousand miles away or at least have gone to her room to be alone instead. Her position and responsibility, though, demanded that she stay with the children until they were in their own beds. So, she stood up, took off her apron and straightened her dress, and obediently went into the library.

With the dishes in the dishwasher and the table and counters cleaned, Matt and Heather prepared a tray for their TV-viewing refreshments. Heather suggested that they make hot chocolate instead of having soda since the evening was cold from the damp fog that now enveloped the marina. And besides, Manar had always made it for her whenever she was upset. It had a way of making one feel relaxed.

The popcorn gave off its enticing aroma as the two entered the library, causing Manar to turn around. She seemed a little calmer and had been laughing at a rerun of a sitcom on TV.

The room was dim, lit only by the glow from the television and the crackling fire in the fireplace.

The three of them settled in on the sofa, the children on either side of Manar with the large velvet throw wrapped around their laps. Manar had the popcorn bowl on her lap, and they all held their mugs of hot chocolate.

Manar had relented, allowing them to watch *Jurassic Park*; it was so engrossing they hardly moved from their comfortable spots. Manar was intently focused on the movie and had forgotten, at least for the time being, about her husband. If someone had been looking at them through the television screen, they would have seen three dimly lit faces, eyes wide open staring at the TV, moving only enough to stuff popcorn in their mouths or take a sip of their hot beverage.

Every now and then Heather would grab Manar's arm with her free hand in response to a frightening scene, and Manar would wrap her arm around Heather to comfort her. And so, the three of them passed the hours until the movie's end. "Whooa, that was great!" Matt said. "Can we watch another movie?"

"Not a scary one though, Matt," Heather insisted.

"How about *Back to the Future*?" Matt said. Aunt Estelle allowed the children to have a small collection of videotapes, which they were allowed to watch only after all their homework had been completed and when there was nothing "intelligent or educational" on television.

"OK," Manar said. "But that'll be the last one and then the two of you have to go to bed."

"Great! Thanks. I'll go get it, it's in my room," Matt said, and he was out from his position on the sofa and almost through the library doors.

"Your room? What's it doing there?" Manar asked.

"I was just reading the jacket cover," Matt yelled back from the hallway.

Matt climbed the staircase and was on his way to his room when something caught his attention. He had seen something out of the corner of his eye. It was in his aunt's bedroom—that was unusual, because normally, the door would have been shut. Matt slowed down and glanced in. The room was dark and Matt shrugged, about to continue on to his own room when he saw a flicker. There *was* something! Someone was in the bedroom and whoever it was had a small pen light. Maybe it was a cat burglar—Matt had seen one in a movie once.

Matt debated whether or not he should go in and confront the intruder. Or should he call 911? As unwise as it was, without further thought, Matt began tiptoeing into his aunt's room. "Who's there?" he said. "What do you want?"

Matt heard fumbling and a stumble and saw the small light beam fall to the floor, followed by the soft thud of the flashlight landing on the carpet. It lay there, casting its triangular glow across the pile. Matt knelt on one knee near the light and was about to pick it up when a large narrow shoe stepped on his hand. "OUCH!" Matt yelled out, grabbing his aching hand, and as he did, he saw a tall shadowy figure run past him. Matt attempted to tackle the intruder but missed and landed on his empty arms instead.

He gathered himself up and ran after the man. "Stop! Help! Manar, call 911! There's a burglar in the house!" Matt shouted at the top of his lungs.

By now both Manar and Heather had heard the commotion and were in the foyer looking up at Matt at the top of the staircase. "What's going on?" Manar asked.

"Didn't you see him run down the stairs? Someone was in Aunt Estelle's room. I saw him and he ran out," Matt said breathlessly, more from his nervousness than from his exertion.

"No. No one came running down," Manar said.

"Uh-uh," Heather grunted, nodding her head in agreement.

"What's all the commotion?" said a craggily voice from the kitchen doorway. It was The Crypt Keeper. He stood there smoothing his hair with his hands and straightening his collar as though he had just been through something strenuous.

51

Chapter 12

No one had told the children of their parents' discovery of the biomarkers for intelligence. It seems their aunt and all the lawyers involved in their parents' legal matters thought it best to wait until Matt turned eighteen. So, neither of the children knew why their parents were on the Cyprus Freeway when it collapsed on October 17th in the 1989 earthquake. But the truth is, Jon and Josie Townsend had been on their way to an appointment with a patent attorney to secure their rights to their major new discovery.

Fortunately, Matt and Heather had been safe with Manar in their home in the Burlingame hills on that fateful day when the earthquake hit. And, even though the house shook violently and the earth seemed to be mad at something or someone, no one was hurt and the house sustained little damage. So, after the death of their parents, it was determined that the children would live with their great-aunt, and the Burlingame house was put on the market and sold quickly.

Fortunately for Roger Hill, with Jon and Josie Townsend's death, he had gotten an ill-deserved reprieve from the legal action Jon Townsend had threatened him with for his covert photocopying of the secret process. And fortunately for him too, Jon Townsend's lab book, documenting a daily record of everything that had transpired, had been sealed and held in probate, along with other personal documents. So, Roger was confident no one would find out about the photocopying incident.

Roger Hill decided to stay on in his position as head of security at SafGen after the Townsends' death. He suspected that a copy of the paper documenting their process was probably shoved in the back of a drawer, forgotten, or somewhere in a bookcase at the firm's facilities. His plan was to get his hands on it. It would be worth millions to the right people. And so, for the next few months he took every opportunity to search the lab and offices, but to his disappointment, uncovered nothing.

It came as no surprise to anyone when SafGen was bought out by a larger biotechnical firm, and no surprise when some of the company's employees had been laid off as a result. Roger was stunned, though, to find that he would be one of those being fired, and very disappointed that the new owners wouldn't want to continue his employment and utilize his expertise. But he finally resigned himself to the fact, and decided that if he were ever to make millions it would have to be through some other means than the secret sale of the coveted process—a process truly worth millions to some devious group hoping to get its hands on it for their own evil purposes.

The next few months found Roger working odd jobs. He had submitted his resume to other biotechnical firms, but none were hiring at the moment. His savings account was emptying quickly due to his extravagance. His current wages just couldn't keep up with his spending habits.

Roger bet heavily at the races, and lost. He got into card games, and lost. He invested in shaky business schemes, and lost. He had to do something about his financial situation, and soon.

It was one evening while Roger was sipping coffee at his favorite dinner, reading the *Chronicle*, when a small photo in the lower, right-hand corner of the front page caught his eye. It was a photo of Matt and Heather. Roger wouldn't have paid any attention to it, but the caption read:

Townsend Children Worth Billions.

The words "Townsend" and "billions" sent chills up his spine. Could it be? Were these the children of his would-be nemesis? He read the full article:

> Young Mathew and Heather Townsend are the heirs of Jon and Josie Townsend, founders of SafGen, Inc., Burlingame, California. With the recent sale of the company, it is speculated that the children may be the youngest billionaires in the country.

> Some suspect that the senior Townsends had discovered the genetic biomarkers for intelligence (see article "Creating Intelligent Babies, Science or Science Fiction," *Chronicle*, April 9, 1989). It appears the world won't know the truth of the matter for some time, though. Because of their untimely deaths in the Loma Prieta earthquake a little over two years ago, the senior Townsends' personal effects have been sealed, not to be opened until young Mathew turns eighteen.

> The new owners of SafGen denied knowledge of the research or of any such discovery. "We do conduct research, but as the company had done under its previous owners, we contract our services out to other firms and none of our clients have indicated an interest in such research," said the company spokesperson, Tom Mead, head of public relations.

The article concluded with:

> The young Townsends are wards of the renowned Mrs. Estelle Furgeson of San Francisco's exclusive Marina District. Mrs. Furgeson is the surviving spouse of Mr. Hubert Furgeson of the United States Diplomatic Service, who was aboard Korean Airlines, Flight 007 when it crashed in 1979.

Roger Hill put the paper down. He hadn't noticed, but the surprise of the article was such a shock that he wasn't holding his cup of coffee properly any longer. Instead, the cup was dangling from his index finger and coffee was spilling onto the counter and splashing onto his lap.

"Dang," he said and stood up quickly, trying to prevent any more coffee from covering the front of his pants. The other patrons looked at him blankly.

"Oh, I'm sorry, sir. Here, here's a rag," the waiter said, handing Roger a clean towel, mopping up the brown puddle on the counter with another.

"Never mind. It's OK. Thanks anyway. How much do I owe you?" Roger wanted to get out of the hot, crowded coffee shop and into the fresh air. He needed to clear his head. He needed to think.

Roger tossed seven dollars and twenty-three cents on the counter to cover his meal. The waiter picked up the money and said, "Thanks," in a sarcastic tone—Roger hadn't left a tip for his services.

Walking in the cold, damp air of the San Francisco night did clear Roger Hill's head. He began devising a plan immediately. Now he realized how fortunate he was to have a job as a night-duty security guard. It was an easy job. It would give him time to plot things out precisely. And it would leave his days open for searching the neighborhood for the house the children lived in. *Where was it?* he asked himself. He stopped under the glow of a streetlight and opened the folded newspaper. *Yeah, the Marina District.* "That shouldn't be too difficult," he whispered under his breath.

Roger's mind started racing. He imagined a copy of the research paper hidden in the house where the children lived with their great aunt. "If there isn't a copy of the paper, there's probably a key to a safe deposit box," he said out loud. Either way, he'd have to get his hands on one or the other. Finally, a way out of his rut and on to wealth.

Roger Hill's current employer was a biotech firm in South San Francisco, and being a night guard there allowed him limited access to security files. He felt confident enough in his own intelligence, though, to be able to access any information he wanted. He would specifically look for files of foreign clients or investors. If he found the right one, he knew he could broker a deal to sell them the illicit information.

Chapter 13

Several weeks had passed since the intruder incident, and it had all but been forgotten. Matt hadn't forgotten though. He had an ill feeling about it. There had been no evidence to suggest that anyone had broken into the house. But Matt knew his senses hadn't deceived him, he had witnessed *someone* rummaging around in his aunt's bedroom. He decided to remain silent about the matter and quietly figure things out.

If no one had broken into the house, then someone on the inside had to have done the rummaging. Manar and Heather had been downstairs watching television, and he had gone to look for the video of *Back to the Future*. That left—THE CRYPT KEEPER. But The Crypt Keeper had said he had other important things to do. *And everyone thought he had left the house.* "Was that what he wanted everyone to think?" Matt whispered to himself. It was certainly suspicious that he suddenly appeared in the foyer and out of breath, and at that precise moment. The more Matt thought about it the more it seemed to be too coincidental. *But why would he be rummaging around Aunt Estelle's bedroom? What was he after? Aunt Estelle's jewels were kept in a wall safe—The Crypt Keeper knew that. And only Aunt Estelle knew the combination.* This would take some further investigation. Matt decided he'd keep an eye on The Crypt Keeper as much as he could for the next few days.

Chapter 14

Heather asked Matt when he was going to go through the secret passageway again. "You haven't gone down there in over a week. What's up?"

"I've just been waiting for the right time, that's all," Matt answered.

"But yesterday would've been the perfect time. The Crypt Keeper was washing the cars and Manar was doing laundry. They wouldn't have been around to bother us," Heather said logically. "And why have you been sneaking around following The Crypt Keeper? Anyone would think you suddenly liked him or something."

"Me? Like The Crypt Keeper! You've gotta be kidding!" Matt said, shaking his head. "No, he's just been acting strange lately and I wanted to keep an eye on him, that's all."

"Ha. That's a laugh. The Crypt Keeper suddenly acting strange. He's always acted strange. No, there's more to it than that, Matt. What's going on?" Heather demanded.

"OK. I haven't said any more about it. But, I swear I *did* see someone in Aunt Estelle's room that night. And, I think it was The Crypt Keeper."

"How do you know it was him?"

"It's only logical. All the rest of us were accounted for. There was no evidence anyone broke in. We all thought The

Crypt Keeper had left. But what if he hadn't? What if he wanted us to *think* he had left so he could sneak around?" Matt said in a hushed tone, as though he were revealing a mystery bit by bit and didn't want anyone else to hear.

"But what could he possibly want in Aunt Estelle's room? Her jewels are—" Matt put his hand on Heather's arm, stopping her in mid-sentence. "I know, I thought of that. But he's up to something, I just know it. That's why I've been following him."

"And have you seen him do anything stranger than usual?" Heather asked.

"No," Matt said, disappointment in his voice.

"Well, have you asked him straight out?" Heather made it sound as though that would've been the simplest thing to do.

"Oh, sure. I'm gonna ask him if it was him going through Aunt Estelle's drawers. What's he gonna say? 'Yes, son. It was me. I wanted to find your aunt's gold 'cause she doesn't pay me enough.' Heather, don't be silly. He wouldn't admit to anything. He'd deny everything."

"Yeah, I guess you're right. He *is* devious. It probably *was* him. But what could he possibly have been looking for?"

The two sat in silence, thinking. Matt finally gave out a long sigh. "Oh well, we'll just have to keep our eyes on him and hope we catch him snooping around again. Where's Manar?" he asked, changing the subject.

"She's in the kitchen making out a list for The Crypt Keeper. Somehow she got him to agree to pick up a few things for her," Heather answered. "Why?"

"So, he'll be out for a while, and Manar said she wanted to work in the herb garden this morning, right? So, she'll be busy. Do you want to go back down the passageway?"

Heather swallowed hard. Little shocks surged all through her body. She was nervous and thrilled all at once. "Yes, let's do it," she finally said.

They waited for the car to pull away, assuring them that The Crypt Keeper would be gone, for a few hours anyway.

60

Heather felt like an old pro at sliding down the ramp, even though this was only her second time. When she got to the bottom, she quickly stood up, happy to see the library and not the dark, wet marsh she had visited on her first trip through the passageway. But wait. On closer inspection she could see this wasn't at all like the library she was used to in her home.

"See," Matt said, guessing her thoughts. "I told you it was different. But you haven't seen anything yet!" and he pulled her by the arm through the library doors and down the hallway into the kitchen.

As they entered the all-white kitchen, Matt pointed to the view outside. Heather stood there, mesmerized. There were pedestrians in strange attire, horse-drawn carriages, Model-T Fords, *and* the steamships. "Oh my gosh!" was all she could say.

"Told you so," Matt said, matter-of-factly. "I'm hungry, aren't you? It must be past 2:00 in our library. We haven't eaten anything since 11:30, and that wasn't much." Matt looked around the kitchen as Heather remained in the same spot, her eyes glued to the scene outside.

"Ah, cookies!" Matt said, spotting a large crock on the tiled counter. "I wonder if they're as good as Manar's." And he removed the lid and took out a large peanut-butter cookie with its telltale crosshatch markings left by the tines of a fork.

Somehow, those words brought Heather to her senses and she quickly grabbed Matt's arm. "Don't eat that! What if the molecules have been damaged or something?" She remembered reading about such things, or maybe it was on The Learning Channel. In any case, she didn't think it was completely wise to even be visiting another time, let alone eat something from it.

"What could be wrong with it? We're in its time. See, it looks OK." Matt took a long sniff. "And it smells like it was just baked." No sooner was his mouth emptied of the last word when he filled it with a large bite of cookie. It felt solid enough when he first bit into it, and he detected a fleeting taste of peanut butter, but that vanished quickly, along with the morsel, like snow melting on his tongue.

"Whoa, that was strange," he said. "I felt myself bite into the cookie. And I thought I tasted it. But, all of a sudden, it was gone."

"See. I told you. Things are more different here than we realize." Matt somehow knew Heather was right.

They were about to retrace their steps and return to their own library, when they heard something. It sounded like footsteps, but they weren't normal. There was the obvious sound of one shoe hitting the floor, but instead of the sound of the second shoe there was a loud tap, as though someone had hit the floor with the tip of a cane. Thud, tap, THUD, TAP, THUD, TAP—the sound was getting louder *and* closer.

"Someone's here," Heather said, almost in tears. It was scary enough being in another time. Now, they were about to be discovered by someone *from* another time.

"We can't go back now. We'll have to hide until the coast is clear and leave then," Matt said, and put his arm around Heather in the hopes of calming her.

"Hide where?" Heather said with a loud sob.

Matt put his hand gently over Heather's mouth and they both heard the footsteps from the hall stop just outside the kitchen door.

Matt motioned with his head for Heather to follow. She nodded, trying to contain herself as the tears rushed down her cheeks.

Matt opened a large cupboard door, turning the knob slowly to assure it wouldn't squeak. The cupboard was empty and there was enough space for the two of them to hide. Matt silently motioned for Heather to go inside. She hurriedly scooted in. Matt grabbed the edge of the door, pulling it closed behind him as he scooted in close to Heather.

"Hoy, who goes there?" a raspy voice said, and Matt and

Heather heard the unusual cadence of the footsteps continue on into the kitchen.

"Pesky rats! Thought I was rid of yer when I left the ship," the voice said. "Molly, MOLLY! Where is that wench? Never around when she's needed. Need to get more rat poison out 'er them rats'll be eat'n me outta house an' home."

The thud/tap continued on around the kitchen and then suddenly stopped again. "What? What's this? Rats can't do that!" Matt and Heather held their breath; surely they had been discovered. "Blasted girl's forgotten to put the lid on the cookie crock. MOLLY, ON DECK, NOW!" Matt and Heather exhaled quietly. They'd gotten another reprieve.

The voice growled "Aarrgg," and the thud/tap pattern continued again, out the kitchen side door and into the herb garden.

Matt poked his head out of the cupboard. He slowly stood up and looked around. He noticed the Dutch doors leading to the herb garden, and took a quick glance through the open upper leaf. No one was in sight. "Heather, let's go. NOW!"

"Heather quickly crawled out of the small space. She stood up and headed for the doors to the hall. She was trying to walk fast and as quietly as possible. And trying to make herself as narrow as possible, scrunching her shoulders and arms close to her body. That way, if anyone were to come in, they might not notice her.

Matt followed Heather. If he hadn't been anxious, he might have been amused at the sight she made with her shoulders almost touching her ears.

Heather grabbed the doorknob and twisted it slowly, as she had seen Matt do, again, trying not to make a sound. They both looked to the left then the right. The hall was clear.

Heather tiptoed sideways along the edge of the wall and Matt mimicked her. They reached the library—at last. They almost felt safe, but they still had to flip the ramp over and climb the stairs to their library.

Heather stopped—gazing, her mouth open in silence. Matt stood there too, frozen like a twin statue of Heather.

THE RAMP WAS GONE! THERE WAS NO WAY BACK TO SAFETY AND THEIR OWN LIBRARY!

The sound of the thud/tap could be faintly heard again, but the cadence was quicker this time, as though the person making it were running—running through the kitchen. Matt and Heather hoped the footsteps wouldn't be heard coming down the marble hall towards the library doors.

Chapter 15

"What'll we do?" Heather said, controlling the scream welling up in her throat.

Matt could see she was about to really panic this time. He had to think quickly. He was surprisingly calm. His mind went into overdrive and everything seemed to be in slow motion.

OK. When he had discovered the secret door, the ramp was already extended. He hadn't done anything to change that fact. It had been extended each time he went through the passageway. But why wasn't it there now? Did that mean the ramp could be manipulated from some hidden button or something? There wasn't time to find out.

What should he do?

Without further thought, Matt automatically walked to the wall corresponding to the wall in his library where the secret passageway should be. There was easy access to it from *this* library. The furniture was placed away from the wall, so he didn't have to crawl through a tunnel-like space here. The door was hidden from view, though, behind a small settee.

The sound of the rapid thud/tap was getting louder and closer; soon it would be at the library doors.

Matt hurried out from behind the settee and quickly grabbed Heather by the arm. She stumbled backwards, still staring at the spot where the ramp should be extending out from the wall above the fireplace.

Matt glanced at the bone-handled letter opener on a side table and picked it up on the way back to the passageway. His movements were quick and methodical as though he were on automatic pilot. He slid the blade in around to the left. Click. The door opened. Sure enough the mariner's clock was hanging were it was supposed to be. It was shinny with none of the years of tarnish built up yet; it was still new.

Matt set the date to August 7, 1997, and the time to 2:30 p.m. He was able to re-hang the clock on his first attempt. He reached into the darkness for the ramp. It was there. Matt firmly took hold of Heather's shoulders and positioned her on the ledge. He sat behind her tandem style, and gave a push with one hand while trying to close the passage door with the other. They were launched. There was no stopping now. They were either on their way to safety or to their doom.

"Hoy, who goes there? I know what you've been up to. You won't get away with it!" the man with the strange footsteps yelled.

Chapter 16

Heather and Matt landed at the bottom of the ramp right onto the leather hassock, and continued rolling on that until they were abruptly stopped by the sofa, causing them to be hurled onto it, head first.

Matt rolled over and sat, staring. Heather rolled over too. Thank goodness! They were safe in their own library. The problem now, though, was their library had a ramp descending from an opening at the top of their fireplace down to the floor. This was terrible. OK, they were safe. But how would they explain the ramp?

Matt got up, exasperated. All he wanted to do was get some milk and cookies and "veg out," as Heather would put it. But, no, he had to solve yet another problem.

Maybe there was a lever on the other side of the ramp that made it collapse back into the wall where it came from. He looked. No lever. He really didn't want to fool around with the lever that made the ramp flip over, revealing the steps; it squeaked too much. But he had no choice. Matt pulled the lever and the ramp creaked and obediently flipped over, revealing the familiar steps. Matt pushed the lever in reverse this time. There was no crack or creak. Instead, as though a well-oiled machine, the steps slowly began receding into midair and into the wall above the fireplace. "Huh," was all

Matt could say, amazed at the cleverness of the whole mechanism.

"Come on, let's get something to eat," he said. And Heather nodded, walking as though she were in a dream and hoped to wake up soon.

When they had finished their snack and felt their nerves settle down, they excused themselves and went back to the library to talk.

"That was too close. I don't think we should visit *that* library again," Heather said.

"Yeah, you're right. That *was* close," Matt agreed.

"Who do you think that was, Matt?"

"It was old Captain Thomas Smyth, the man who built the house." Matt was sure of it.

"Do you think he's going to try and find us by coming to *our* time?"

"No. He was just trying to scare us," Matt said, but he wasn't so sure.

"Why do you think his footsteps sounded so funny, Matt?"

"Because he had a wooden peg for a leg. Like Sam, Aunt Estelle's gardener."

Matt and Heather sat stunned. Their mouths hung open in disbelief. "Do you think he really could've—?" Heather started to ask if Matt thought that Sam and the Old Mariner *were* one and the same person, but Matt stopped her in mid-sentence.

"Yeah. That's what he meant when he said 'I know what you've been up to.'"

For the next few days, both Heather and Matt avoided the secret passageway and went back to watching The Crypt Keeper instead. They were looking for any signs of strange behavior, but The Crypt Keeper was staying within his normal routine around the house and had even become suspiciously polite to them all. The only thing that was a little out of the ordinary was his frequent outings. Instead of an occasional trip out, he now left daily.

"Do you think it was really him rummaging around, Matt? I mean, he hasn't tried to get into Aunt Estelle's room since that night you thought you saw him," Heather said.

"I didn't just think I saw him. It was him. I know it," Matt answered. "Let's just give it more time. He'll try again, I'm sure."

Because The Crypt Keeper's daily excursions had gone from half an hour to an hour, then an hour and a half, and were now over two hours, it had become the new accepted routine. Manar seemed to welcome the respite from his constant nagging, and every morning she would either invite the neighbor's maid, Azita, to come in for tea or visit her next door for refreshments. The two ladies spent the three hours talking about what they remembered about Iran, the country of their births, or about the adjustments to living in a foreign country or about their pride at becoming American citizens.

Matt and Heather began a new routine now too. Every morning after breakfast, they made use of their unencumbered time to go through the secret passageway. At first Heather didn't want to go back. It had been so nerve-racking the last time.

"Come on, Heather," Matt insisted. "We agreed our life was boring and that we wanted adventure. Well, now we've got it. There's bound to be risks—that's what makes it so exciting. Would you rather go back to the way things were?"

"Yes," Heather said meekly, but quickly recanted with a "No, no. It was boring before. You're right."

So, their routine included donning fanny packs with snacks and water, as if they were about to begin a long expedition.

They had even begun experimenting more with the knobs of the mariner's clock to manipulate what time they would visit. Tired with visiting the past, they attempted a visit to the future. The furniture there was like none they had seen before, and the lighting seemed to glow from no particular source. Looking out the windows they saw strange vehicles and water craft that hovered above the street and water. While there were some people in this time that still walked, most were on strange platforms, suspended in midair but moving steadily along.

So far Matt and Heather had had no further encounter with any other human, past or future—and they liked it that way. They weren't sure how they'd deal with another human face to face from a different time than their own, or how that human might deal with them.

"I wish we could set the time just right to visit the library when Mommy and Daddy were here visiting Aunt Estelle?" Heather said wistfully.

"I don't think Mom and Dad visited Aunt Estelle much, but we could try setting the time to when they were still alive and go to our old home in Burlingame," Matt answered.

"Oh, could we, Matt? Please?" Heather delighted in the idea. She didn't know if she'd ever want to leave if she could see her parents again.

"I don't think we should let them see us if we ever succeed in getting the timing right, though. It might be too much of a shock," Matt said, wondering what the effect would be on both he and his sister to see their parents alive and well and not dare talk to them, let alone appear before them.

Heather agreed. "All I want to do is see Mommy and Daddy again, that's all." But, deep down, she knew she really wished she could be in their arms for the rest of eternity. And, the emotion of that thought caused her eyes to well up with tears.

"OK, let's plan for tomorrow then," Matt said. "We'll get our packs ready today and stuff them behind the sofa. That way we'll be ready to leave as soon as The Crypt Keeper pulls out of the driveway. That should give us enough time to get through the passageway, get to Burlingame, spend abut half an hour there, and return, hopefully with some time to spare.

Let's research the bus and train routes from here to Burlingame today, and make sure we have enough money for all the fares."

"Right," Heather said. "I've got some money in my drawer I was saving for some stickers. I don't know if it's enough but it'll help."

"I've got some too. We'll pool it together. We'll have enough. I'll get on the computer to see if I can get the routes and fares."

They planned all afternoon. Matt's research paid off. They'd get on the #45 MUNI bus a few short blocks away, near the Palace of Fine Arts. They'd take that to the CalTrain depot at Fourth and King Streets. Once on the CalTrain commuter, it would be a short ride to the Burlingame depot. Then it would just be an even shorter ride on a taxi to their old house.

Neither of them got much sleep that night. The anticipation of their trip made them nervous and excited all at once.

Chapter 17

Roger Hill smiled smugly to himself as he drove to his regular morning meeting. He was pleased with his own cleverness and his success at finally connecting with someone who was interested in buying the information on the biomarkers for intelligence.

He didn't care if the would-be buyer didn't want to create a race of intelligent babies, but was interested, instead, of genetically manipulating DNA to create a race of *obedient* babies.

The potential buyer's servant, Rashi, almost looked like a duplicate of Roger, except that his skin was much darker and he was much shorter. "My master will have a civilization which listens to reason, which obeys the laws without question, which is moral and clean. Enough of what has been. The future will be orderly! He will see to it that it is!" the odd man had told Roger.

Roger didn't really like Rashi, nor his master, Abdula Robdala, for that matter. Both were overly polite and condescending. But, a business deal was a business deal. And besides, he'd have enough money to live the way he wanted, wherever he wanted. He wasn't going to have any children, so what did he care. "And, besides, everyone dies eventually," he told himself. "So, by the time this guy's created *his brave new world full of obedient zombies* I'll be long gone and won't have to deal with it anyway." *The people in that world would just have to manage. If their brains had been manipulated, they wouldn't know what was going on anyway,* he thought.

So, Roger had justified everything to himself. He just hoped he could find the research paper soon. The sooner he could find it, the sooner he could sell it. And the sooner he'd have the money and wouldn't have to deal with these lunatics any longer.

If anything, Roger enjoyed the ride through Marin County. The modest but beautiful house nestled in the hills of Kentfield was a pleasant place for his monthly meeting with Abdula Robdala, better than the dingy cafes and dirty corners where he met daily with Rashi.

"Well, Mr. Hill, have you been successful yet? Our patience is growing thin. You promised success months ago but have yet to deliver anything," Abdula Robdala said.

"I told Rashi—I almost got caught last time, so I've had to be careful. But I've checked almost the entire house, there are only a few more spots left—"

Abdula Robdala interrupted Roger. "Only a few more spots left. And what if you come up empty-handed, Mr. Hill? What am I to do then?" and he placed his hand on his hip, pushing his long robe aside. A small dagger glistened from the glow of a nearby lamp.

"I'll have it for you in a month," Roger found himself saying, almost as though he were hypnotized by his host. If he had thought about it, he would have known there would have been no way for him to guarantee success.

"All right, Mr. Hill, I'll hold you to that," Abdula Robdala said, in a sickeningly sweet voice. "Now, shall we enjoy our refreshments," he added, holding his chest with one hand while making a slight bow, and pointing the way into the adjoining room with the other hand.

Stupid, stupid! Roger thought to himself on his way back home. *You've only got one month. What made you open your stupid mouth and say that anyway? But,* he thought with a brief moment of bravery, *what's he gonna do if I don't get it?* A queasy feeling suddenly hit the pit of Roger Hill's stomach as he remembered the glint of the dagger in Abdula Robdala's waistband. He'd better find that paper, and soon!

Chapter 18

The fog-shrouded, morning sunlight cast an eerie glow in the room. Matt slowly opened his eyes from a peaceful dream and looked at the clock. *Oh my gosh*, he thought, *it's eight o'clock. We've gotta get mov'n.*

He got up and went into the adjoining bathroom, and opened the door leading into Heather's room. "Heather, Heather. Wake up. We've gotta get going if we want to leave by nine."

Heather slowly opened her eyes. She had been deep in the middle of a dream about her mom and dad. She smiled and looked up at Matt. "What, Mommy? Do I have to get up already?" She was obviously not fully awake yet.

"Come on, Heather. Wake up. It's eight. We wanted to leave by nine so we'll have enough time to go to Burlingame and back before anyone misses us."

"Huh? Oh, OK," Heather said as she threw off the covers.

They had both bathed the night before, so all they had to do was get dressed and have breakfast.

Early on, Matt had made some excuse to Manar about helping Heather with a project for the science fair for the next school term. That way, he reasoned, no one would be suspicious about all the time they were spending in the library. Matt claimed Heather wanted to get a jump on the rest of her classmates, and since she was a little weak in science, it would give her an added boost.

Matt and Heather hurried through breakfast, ran up to their bathroom, brushed their teeth, and raced down the staircase to the library.

It was already 9:10 a.m. The Crypt Keeper had left over ten minutes ago. Matt was glad he had allowed only two hours for their trip through time. That would leave them time enough for little mishaps and to get back before being discovered. If they had slept much later, they would have had to have scrapped the trip for another day.

Matt set the date on the mariner's clock to August 26, 1989, at 7:45 in the morning. He had done a thorough search on the Internet to find out what days in August would fall on a Saturday. That way he knew both of their parents would be home, and their chances of seeing them would be greater.

"OK, Heather. It's set. Ready?"

"Yes," Heather answered, nervous and excited.

Whoosh. Down the ramp they slid, Matt behind Heather. They landed in the library of 1989. It looked pretty much the same as the current one, and they guessed that at this date their aunt was probably somewhere in Europe on her annual trip.

"OK, let's hurry," Matt said. "If there are servants here we don't want them to see us. They won't know who we are and might call the police to report two suspicious children mysteriously showing up in the house. That could be disastrous!"

They hurried to the double library doors and peeked out, looking to the left then the right—so far, so good. They hurriedly tiptoed through the hall, past the staircase and to the large entry doors. They were through the entry and down the steps onto Marina Boulevard in no time. They turned left and, even though there was probably enough time, they ran all the way to the Palace of Fine Arts, and turned left again to Lyon Street and the MUNI stop.

76

They made it just in time to see the bus coming towards them from about a block away.

The bus pulled up to the stop and Heather read the number on the marquee. "This is the number 45, is that the one we want?"

"Yes, this is it," Matt answered. As they boarded the bus, Matt glanced at the clock on the dash board; it read 9:05. Matt told Heather to set her watch to the same time. That way they could keep track of what hour it would be in this dimension so as not to exceed the two hours he had allotted for their travels. With his watch set to their time, they would also know what time it was there as well.

They sat scrunched together on the seat so they could both stare out the window. This was the first time they had spent more than just an hour exploring through the secret passage, and for the fist time Heather noticed that everything seemed a little odd.

"Everything looks kind of strange. Like it's not really solid," Heather observed.

"It's probably just the dirty window," Matt said. But he noticed how people and objects seemed to be more like holographic projections than made of real substance. He didn't want to say anything to Heather though. She'd probably really freak out. And he certainly didn't want that!

Time travel had made them keenly aware of their surroundings, unlike everyone else who only halfheartedly paid attention to what was happening around them. If they *would* have paid attention, Matt and Heather would have seemed as though they were holographic projections too.

The bus finally pulled up to Fourth and King Streets and the driver announced, "CalTrain Depot."

"This is our stop, Heather, now we just have to catch the train."

They boarded the train and paid the fare to Burlingame to the conductor. Neither had ridden in a train before and the experience of it added to their adventure.

Matt asked Heather what the time was on her watch. "It's already 9:40," she said.

"I hope we'll be able to get a taxi quickly and get to our old house. There isn't much time left—we still have the reverse trip back to our house and then up the ramp to our own library—hopefully, without being seen," Matt said seriously.

"YES!" Matt almost shouted when he saw the line of taxi cabs near the train stop. He hailed one, giving the driver their destination on the way in.

The old neighborhood was beautiful and memories of their life there flooded Matt and Heather's minds. Tears filled both their eyes. Matt cleared his throat and wiped his eyes with the sleeve of his fleece jacket. "Here, this is it. Ahh, could you pull over to the other side of the street and wait for us? We'll only be a little while. Thanks?"

"Sure, young man. I'll wait a little while," the taxi driver answered. He was impressed by the maturity of his two young fares.

Matt and Heather got out and looked both ways down the street as the taxi pulled around. They ran across and into their old driveway. The giggles of children could be heard about two houses down. "Let's hurry. We don't want to be seen by anyone," Matt said.

They slipped through the side gate and hid in the bushes near the kitchen window, and peeked in. Sitting there was their dad drinking coffee as he had done every Saturday morning, still in his robe, reading the morning paper. Their mom was standing at the stove making her usual scrambled eggs and bacon.

Tears flooded Matt and Heather's eyes again. "Mommy—" Heather called out. She was about to run into the house and to her mother when Matt put his hand over her mouth. They both sat there sobbing in each other's arms.

"What dear, what's the matter?" Mom had heard Heather's call and was walking into the family room in response.

"We've got to go *now*," Matt said.

"No. No! I don't want to. I don't ever want to go."

"It's OK, Heather. We'll be back," Matt said, trying to calm himself as well as his sister.

With his arm still around her shoulders, Matt gently guided her out from the bushes and into the street to the waiting cab.

"What's wrong, little miss?" the cab driver said. Heather couldn't respond, she was sobbing too much.

"It's our old house," Matt said. "We had to move. But we missed it so much we had to see it again."

"Oh, I know, it can be tough moving. But I'm sure your parents had a good reason." Those words only caused Heather to sob even harder. "Don't worry, little miss. Once you settle into your new home you'll forget all about this one."

They finally reached the CalTrain Depot. "Thanks. How much do we owe you?" Matt said.

"That'll be sixteen dollars and sixty cents, young man," the driver said.

"Thanks," Matt said, and handed the man a twenty-dollar bill. "Keep the change," he added, knowing that when he and Heather got back to their own time, the money they were spending would be back, almost as if by magic.

"Thank you, young sir," the driver said, thinking Matt was more generous at his young age than some adult fares he had had. "Take care, little miss." Heather nodded, and gave the driver a faint smile. She had finally clamed down, but her eyes were red and swollen.

Matt and Heather made it safely back home. The total trip time had taken them two hours and fifteen minutes. Matt made note of that while Heather changed her watch back to their current time.

Chapter 19

"I've been thinking a lot about it, Matt. I don't think it was the dirty windows that made everyone look strange on our trip to our old house," Heather whispered in the back seat of the Lincoln Town Car. The Crypt Keeper had uncharacteristically agreed to drive everyone to Muir woods for a picnic. Matt guessed he was trying to cover up something with his accommodating behavior. If he had given it more thought, he would have realized The Crypt Keeper was just covering himself. He would tell Madame Furgeson that he had taken everyone on a pleasant drive to the national park when she asked how their summer went.

"I think you're right," Matt whispered back. "Everything looked as though it were a holographic projection or something."

"Do you think it's that way because it's not our own time?"

"Yeah, probably."

"You know what else?" Heather said. "We're going to have to come up with some science project. We haven't done anything yet, and Aunt Estelle's due home soon. She'll want to know what we've done all summer. Manar will surely mention that we've spent a lot of time working on some sort of project." Heather had obviously given it a lot of serious thought.

"Yeah, you're right. We can throw something together, though. When we get home we'll start working on it."

The picnic had been pleasant enough, and the smell of the pines and firs in the forest was refreshing and relaxing. Manar had wrapped her arms through The Crypt Keeper's and had even put her head on his shoulder as they sat on the picnic bench. Looking at the two of them, one would have thought nothing had ever been wrong and that they were both thoroughly in love with one another.

After about an hour and a half The Crypt Keeper abruptly stood up and said it was time to get back, breaking Manar's reverie.

When they got home, Matt asked Manar where he might find a board for Heather's science project.

"Look in the garage," she said. "There's probably something out there you could use."

"I'll go with you," Heather said.

Matt flipped on the light switch. The garage was dimly lit and smelled musty. The walls were made of rough-hewn stones and the ceiling had huge timbers as supports. Along the walls were free-standing metal shelving. The two of them looked around the periphery of the garage, but couldn't find any board to work as a platform for their mock science project. "Maybe there's something in the gardening shed. I don't see anything here we can use," Heather said.

"Whoa, what's this?" Matt said. Heather knelt in the corner next to Matt to get a better look at what he had discovered. There, on the bottom shelf, was a stack of old ledgers. Some of the labels on the outside covers read *SafGen*.

"SafeGen?" Heather said. "Isn't that the name of—?"

"Yes," Matt said. "But look at this."

He had flipped through one of the ledgers; stuck in the middle was a photograph. Its caption read, *Members of the SafGen Staff.* And it went on to list the names of each individual in the photograph.

"Oh, that's a nice picture of Mommy and Daddy," Heather said. "Let's take it out."

"Look closer," Matt said. "Look at this guy," and he pointed to the man to the right of their father.

"Huh? No. No way," Heather said in astonishment.

"Yes, way," Matt said. "Look there," he added, pointing to the name. "It says, *Roger Hill, head of security.*"

Chapter 20

Heather had finally become as suspicious of The Crypt Keeper as Matt. The man *was* devious and it was no coincidence that he lived in the same house as they. No wonder he had been so polite to their aunt from the very beginning. He had manipulated his way in. He *was* looking for something—but what?

Matt and Heather had completed the mock science project in no time using a discarded masonite board they found in the gardening shed. The project was a demonstration of a volcano. They had downloaded some graphics from the Internet showing a cross section of a volcano with its strata of magma and molten lava. They placed that, along with a written description of an eruption and lava flow, on a tri-fold, cardboard backdrop. Below that sat the board with the mockup of a volcano they had made from a flour-and-water paste. The whole thing was very ingenious, especially for something that wasn't really a requirement at school. Heather decided that rather than let the whole thing go to waste, though, she would share it with her classmates. They'd be impressed with the little eruption of vinegar and baking soda spurting out the top. The only task left was to add paint, giving it a more realistic look.

It took them a total of only three hours to complete the whole project, but that was over a period of two weeks. Matt and Heather had abandoned their trips through the secret passage for the time being, thinking it more important to work on the project instead and keep a close eye on The Crypt Keeper when they could.

"I only wish we could follow him wherever he goes each morning," Matt said. "I'll bet it has something to do with his rummaging around Aunt Estelle's bedroom."

"Do you think she's in danger, Matt?"

"I don't know. But if *she's* in danger, we're probably *all* in danger."

"Should we tell Aunt Estelle we saw him rummaging through her things?"

"No, it won't do any good. We have no proof. Let's just hope he tries something again—soon."

Aunt Estelle had returned at the end of August. She was all aflutter about what social events she had attended and of her renewed friendships with her European friends, and how the Riviera was such a delight each summer.

She brought her usual snow globes for everyone and was pleased with the deliberate excitement they all displayed at opening the boxes, all but Matt. *Why did everyone pretend to be surprised by the gifts? Wasn't it the same routine, year after year? Aunt Estelle would go on her annual jaunt, enjoying herself. Then, when she got back everyone would squeal at the contents of the square boxes, even though every year it would be the same old thing.* Matt had forgotten that when he was younger he enjoyed receiving the mementos as much as everyone else. In fact, he had his collection displayed in the bookcase in his bedroom just the same as Heather. But his disappointment was even stronger when he realized the one he received this year was a duplicate of the one Aunt Estelle had given him last year. *Oh well, that was unimportant. They all deserved their moment of joy,* Matt thought to himself. *Danger was probably looming before them all.*

Late one night, not quite a week after Aunt Estelle had

returned, Matt remembered he had left his pocket knife in the library alongside the science project. It had been the perfect tool to shape the volcano. The knife had been his father's scout knife, and even though Matt wasn't allowed to carry it, he kept it in his desk drawer and used it on little projects, such as his model planes.

The house was dark except for the thin strips of light that glowed beneath the bedroom doors lining the hallway. Everyone had settled in for the evening, reading or watching television before going to sleep.

Matt tiptoed so as not to alert anyone that he was up and about. In his haste he had forgotten about the squeaky step at the top of the stairwell, though, and the sound in the still night seemed to eco down the hallway. Matt clinched his teeth and closed his eyes, hoping no one had heard. He stood there for a moment. Weeew, it was safe to continue on.

Matt stepped onto the marble floor in the foyer. It was cold. He had forgotten to put on his slippers. He hurried across the floor on the tips of his toes, not wanting to feel the full impact of the cold on his bare feet. His footsteps made almost no sound.

As he quietly strode across the foyer floor, he suddenly realized how easy it was to see. At first he had thought it was the night light. But the night light was in the upstairs hallway, not the foyer.

Matt stared. Reflecting off the shiny marble tiles was a thin beam of light emanating from beneath the library doors. Someone was in the library. The lights wouldn't have been left on by accident. As butler, it was The Crypt Keeper's duty to make sure everything was shut off and that the house was locked down each night.

This could only mean one thing. Someone *was* in the library—and that someone most certainly was The Crypt Keeper!

Matt hurried the remaining distance to the library doors and threw them open.

So engrossed in his task, The Crypt Keeper hadn't heard Matt's footsteps. It was the sound of the doors opening that had startled him. He sat there, crouched, looking like a night predator that had suddenly been discovered hovering over its prey. His eyes were wide in surprise and they shone yellow in the dim light. He was to the right of the fireplace, in front of the library shelves, and he held a book he had been flipping through. Several books lay strewn around him like discarded bits of bone taken from a carcass.

"What're you up to? I'm going to call Aunt Estelle," Matt said. He hadn't yelled, but he hadn't whispered either.

The Crypt Keeper didn't know what to do. Matt admittedly had the upper hand.

Matt stood there with his hands on his hips and had positioned his feet wide apart so as to plant himself firmly in position.

The Crypt Keeper stood up slowly to his full height. Even though Matt was much shorter, his stance gave him the air of a general. He was in command of *this* situation. The Crypt Keeper was obviously intimidated, but he was thinking and an expression of self-satisfaction slowly crept across his face.

"Master Mathew," he said in an assured tone. "What are *you* doing out of *your* bedroom? I believe it is *I* who should be speaking to Madam Furgeson. Isn't tomorrow your first day back to school? I think Madame would be quite upset if she knew you were up and about and not asleep as you should be."

"Don't change the subject," Matt said defiantly. "You're up to something. I know more than you think I do, and I'm going to tell Aunt Estelle." Matt's determination threw The Crypt Keeper off guard, and Matt wasn't going to back down.

"What do you think you know, Master Mathew?" The Crypt Keeper said, hedging his bet that Matt was just bluffing.

"Never mind, I'll save what I know for Aunt Estelle." Matt

was mad. His heart was pounding and he found it hard to breathe, spurting out each sentence between gulps of air.

"Answer my question. What have you been looking for? It was you who was in Aunt Estelle's room and I'm going to tell her that."

A smile spread across The Crypt Keeper's face. *You know nothing, little man,* he thought, not yet realizing how much Matt *did* know.

Even though the television set Aunt Estelle had been watching was effective at casting its hypnotic glare causing her to doze, she awoke at the sound of Matt's staccato shouts coming from downstairs. She shut off the television, threw on her robe, and ran down the staircase shouting for Roger to come help.

Aunt Estelle was surprised to see The Crypt Keeper and Matt standing facing one another, apparently in deep discussion.

"What are you doing out of bed—and on a weeknight? Mathew, I'm speaking to you. And, Roger, I'm surprised at you—indulging a child in foolish banter when he should be in bed."

"Madame, that is just what I have been saying to Master Mathew. I came downstairs to double check the locks and I found him here on the floor going through those books," The Crypt Keeper said, pointing a boney finger at the pile that lay on the floor.

Matt stood there with his mouth gaping. *What nerve!*

"Mathew, to bed, now. We'll discuss this matter tomorrow, after school. I'll decide then what punishment you'll receive. And, to think, I've only been back for a few days and you welcome me home with this behavior."

She turned in a dramatic twirl, her robe fanning out like a dancer's ball gown. "Roger, please replace those books and see Mathew to his room. Goodnight to you both," and Estelle Furgeson strode out the library doors with an air of righteous indignation.

The Crypt Keeper looked down at Matt with a sinister grin. He knew he needn't say a word.

All right, Matt thought. *You've won this battle, but the war's not over yet.* And he walked out of the room with as much dignity as he could muster.

Chapter 21

On that sunny, Saturday morning in 1989, Josie Townsend walked into the family room of her Burlingame home. "What, Heather darling? Did you call Mommy?"

"No, Mommy, I didn't call you. But look out the window. Two kids ran out of that yellow car, and now there's a strange man sitting in it looking at our house."

"Oh, that's just a taxi, honey; he's probably waiting to take someone to the airport. Remember when we rode in one on our vacation? Daddy paid the driver to take us to our hotel room. Maybe Manar can find the little book about cars and read to you about taxis while Mommy finishes breakfast, OK?"

Little Heather got bored with the story about taxis—her mother's explanation had been enough to satisfy her. Instead, she quickly found the book about bunnies and had Manar read that.

By the time Josie Townsend had called everyone in for breakfast, Heather had completely forgotten about the two children she had seen and about the taxi.

Chapter 22

At lunch the next noon following the incident in the library, Matt explained to Heather how he had caught The Crypt Keeper crouching over the strewn books. "—and he looked like a mad predator hovering over them that way." Then, after a slight pause Matt added, "That man's clever, I'll give him that. Now *I'm* the one who has to get punished."

By the time Matt and Heather had gotten home that afternoon, though, Aunt Estelle had forgotten about the incident and the punishment, and Matt assumed he was home free. It was only later at dinner, when The Crypt Keeper said through a smirk while serving Mrs. Ferguson, "Madam, might I give a suggestion?"

"Yes, of course, Roger, what is it?"

"If you haven't already given Master Mathew his punishment, Madam, perhaps his help with washing and polishing the cars this Saturday would suffice."

At first Aunt Estelle sat, staring blankly. Then it came to her. *Oh, yes, the punishment.*

"I think that's a splendid idea." With a broad smile she addressed Matt as though the idea had been hers all along. "Mathew, for your punishment you shall help Roger wash and polish both cars."

The dumb smirk was etched into The Crypt Keeper's face as he feigned politeness and asked Matt if he wanted seconds.

"No, thank you," Matt answered gruffly.

Heather had been about to take her next bite when this whole scene began playing out. Now she sat there with her fork in midair watching Matt's reaction.

Saturday had come and gone, but the memory of how The Crypt Keeper delighted in giving him orders infuriated Matt. He had to wash the cars twice because he supposedly hadn't done it right the first time. He knew it was The Crypt Keeper's way of getting revenge and of putting Matt in his place.

On Sunday, Aunt Estelle had been invited to brunch at the Palace Hotel's Garden Court restaurant, and as chauffer, The Crypt Keeper had to drive her. Manar said she wasn't feeling well and went back to her room to nap. That gave Matt and Heather most of the afternoon to themselves.

"I'm going to do some exploring through the passageway. I'd invite you to go, but you'd probably find it boring this time," Matt said.

"No, that's OK. I really don't want to go anyway. I'd rather go out to the garden and read," Heather answered, not knowing where Matt was really headed.

Matt donned his backpack, said goodbye to Heather, and scooted behind the sofa. Now that he was out of sight, he checked to see that he had enough money for the trip. He opened the passageway door, adjusted the timepiece, and slid down the ramp. The trip to Burlingame seemed to go quicker now that he was making it alone. He used the quiet time to figure out how he would explain his presence to his father, and he was glad he didn't have to worry about Heather's reaction to seeing their old house and parents again.

Matt had set the date and time to the evening of October 12, 1989. His child self would be with his mom at a Mom and Son Bingo Fundraiser for the PTA. If Matt had remembered correctly, they would both be gone for most of the evening. He remembered the date well because it was the first time Heather was gone from home too to spend the evening at a sleepover with a friend. Mom had made a fuss that her babies were growing up too fast. Dad would be home alone. Matt's plan had been in the works for days. He wanted to be alone with his father. His dad was the only one he could turn to. He had to get him to understand what was happening and hopefully figure out why The Crypt Keeper sought employment as butler and chauffer to Aunt Estelle.

By the time he reached the front door to his old house, Matt had decided to pass himself off as the substitute paper boy, collecting payment for the deliveries. He just hoped the real paper boy hadn't already been there.

Jon Townsend opened the door with a smile. He was clutching his log book and his reading glasses were slung low on the bridge of his nose. Matt had almost forgotten how comical his dad looked peering over them. "Yes, can I help you, young man?" his dad said, staring as though he knew Matt from somewhere.

"Achem," Matt cleared his throat. "I, I'm here to collect for the paper delivery."

"Oh, oh yes. Come in. Gee, uh, I thought Josie paid that last week. Must've misunderstood. Come on in, son. How much do I owe you?" he added as he shoved his hand in his pocket.

Matt fumbled through his mind for an appropriate amount to give when Jon Townsend said, "Do I know you from somewhere, son? You look awfully familiar. I can't get over the uncanny resemblance, but you're a lot older. I've got a very strange feeling—" and Jon Townsend wavered as though he were about to faint.

Matt grabbed his father's arm in an attempt to make contact as well as steady him. "Maybe we'd better go set down."

"Yeah, that's a good idea," his father answered, stumbling into the living room. Jon Townsend slumped into his big easy chair and ran his hand through his hair. "Gosh, I feel strange," he said. "I've never quite felt like this before—like I'm in a dream or something."

Matt sat on the ottoman at the foot of the chair. "Yes, in a way I guess it is like a dream," Matt started out slowly. "I, I look familiar because—I am."

Jon Townsend stared at the young person sitting opposite him.

"I, I'm Mathew," Matt said quietly, hoping his father could digest the information *and* believe it.

"You're who?"

"I'm Mathew and I've—"

Matt was about to explain everything to his father when Jon Townsend stood up abruptly and said in a loud voice, "Now listen here, son, I don't know what you're up to or who you're trying to fool, but—" He stopped in mid-sentence as he looked at the object in the young imposter's hand.

"Do you recognize this?" Matt asked. "It was yours—"

Jon Townsend grabbed the boy scout knife from Matt's hand. "What is this?" he said as he examined it. Recognizing the familiar chip on one edge he added, "How did you get this?"

"That's what I'm trying to explain. It was yours. I inherited it after—" Matt paused. Should he finish the sentence "—*after you died*"? How would someone handle information like that? "Please believe me," Matt started speaking with the shotgun delivery he always used whenever he got excited. "I'm your son. I am Mathew. I haven't got much time to explain. Heather and I live with Great-Aunt Estelle now. The old captain had a secret passage built and there's a mariner's clock hanging at the entrance. The clock is bewitched or something. But, you can set it to any date and travel there. That's how I got here. That's why I look older, because I am."

"Wait a minute. You're telling me you're Mathew, and that you and Heather live with Aunt Estelle? Why are you living with Aunt Estelle?

Matt nodded his head and a broad smile brightened his face. Finally, his dad was beginning to understand what he was saying. Matt was about to continue the explanation.

"OK, son. That's about enough. I think you'd better leave now," Jon Townsend said as he grabbed the boy's arm.

"Wait. Stop. Look at me real hard. Do I look completely solid like everything else in this room? And do I feel completely solid?"

This comment caught Jon Townsend off guard. He looked closely at Matt. Suddenly, he dropped his grip on Matt's arm as though he had been holding something strange.

"Now do you believe me?" Matt said. "What else can I do to prove that what I'm saying is true? I know. Where's *your* boy scout knife? Let's compare the two. If they look exactly alike then wouldn't that prove that I'm from the future?"

As if hypnotized, Jon Townsend went to his desk in the corner. He held up the knife that lay conveniently in the drawer. He had been using it as a letter opener for years and had dropped it on the tiled floor, creating the small chip. Yes, it *was* the same knife, there was no doubt now.

"This is fantastic. I want to know everything. I—" Jon Townsend's scientific mind was in full gear and he was poised to take extensive notes.

"I haven't got much time," Matt said, knowing his dad was convinced now. "I have to get back before they discover I'm gone. Heather and I came here about a little over a month ago to see if we could make it in two hours—"

"You were here before, with Heather? But—"

"Yes, I wanted to wait to get you home alone so I could talk with you without upsetting Mom and baby Heather," Matt continued. "The reason I came here today was to ask you about Roger Hill."

"Roger Hill? He's our head of security at the company. Why?"

"Because he works for Aunt Estelle now, as her butler and chauffer."

"As her butler and chauffer? Ha, ha. What in heaven's name would he be doing as a butler? Ha, that's a good one."

Jon Townsend couldn't imagine his head of security as a butler, although if he thought about it, Roger did look the part.

"Dad, he's been acting stranger than usual lately. I caught him rummaging around in Aunt Estelle's room while she was on her annual trip."

"Well, son, he *is* a strange man. But I trust him. He's been good for our company. He has all the latest security gadgets installed and his team is right on top of everything. No, he's got everything very organized and we have no complaints. You kids just probably get on his nerves. I don't imagine Roger's ever been fond of kids.

"Now, tell me about Heather, and why you're living with Aunt Estelle, and what it's like to time travel? Just think, my kids, time traveling. You're both going to be better scientists than your mom and I put together!"

"Dad, I haven't got time now. I really do have to get back. Would you just watch The Crypt Keeper—I mean Roger, to see if he does anything strange?"

"The Crypt Keeper? That's a pretty unflattering name."

"That's what Heather and I call him. He gave us both the creeps the very first time we saw him. —I've got to go now, Dad. But I'll come back. Promise you won't tell Mom I was here, at least not yet."

"No, I won't tell her. She wouldn't believe me anyway, she'd need proof."

"When will she and Heather be out next? Oh, and I guess the younger me too."

"Wednesday night is parents' night at school. Mom and I were going with you and Heather, but I'll make some excuse to get out of it so I can be home alone. See you then, son."

On the trip back home and to his own time Matt was filled with mixed emotions. He was thrilled to have visited his dad and have an adult-like conversation with him. Once his dad was convinced of the truth he had treated Matt as a colleague rather than just a son.

Matt choked back tears as he imagined all the things they would have done together if his dad had lived. Nevertheless, it was great to have these moments with him, and Matt knew that somehow, in the great scheme of the universe, he had touched the essence of his father and their bond was even stronger than before. But, Matt's purpose for going back was to find out more about Roger Hill—and he hadn't really accomplished that. He just hoped that his next visit would prove more fruitful.

Chapter 23

Meanwhile, during Matt's latest excursion, Heather had positioned herself on the comfortable chaise lounge in the garden. She wanted to enjoy one of the few remaining, rare Indian summer days San Francisco had to offer.

It was pleasant under the shade of the Japanese elm and Heather took in a lungful of the still-blooming sweet William's broom. Her great-aunt's gardener had really done a beautiful job of creating a pleasant hideaway in the city. *Her aunt's gardener! That was Sam, and Matt and she had agreed that Sam and the old mariner were, most likely, one and the same person.* No sooner had Heather finished that thought when Sam appeared, seemingly, out of nowhere. He cast a disparaging eye in her direction, but didn't say a word.

Heather tried to hide behind her book, but she couldn't concentrate and kept peeking over the edge of it to see what Sam was doing. He was trimming the bushes and staring back. Apparently, he hadn't taken his eyes off her the whole time.

As his work brought him closer to Heather's spot, he began talking, as if to himself. "Some kiddies can't mind ther own business. Always sneak'n round, nosing into other people's affairs. Gett'n into things they shouldn't be gett'n into."

"Excuse me?" Heather said. "Were you talking to me, sir?"

"Jus' say'n that some young folks get into things they shouldn't be gett'n into."

"I'm sorry, sir, did Matt and I disturb something in the potting shed?"

"Don't know. Did'je?"

"I don't think so, Mr. Sam. We tried to be careful."

"Careful, were ye. Ye aren't always careful though, are ye?"

"What do you mean?" Heather had a sick feeling in the pit of her stomach and all sorts of thoughts were flashing through her mind. *Was Sam about to confront her about her and Matt's visit to the old mariner's house and time?*

Sam interrupted her thoughts. "This 'ouse's special and it were built by special 'ands. It weren't meant to be toyed with." He was speaking as though the house were a living entity, not an inanimate object.

"I'm sorry, I, I'm not sure I understand what you're referring to."

"Oh, I think ye know very well what I'm speak'n 'bout, missy." And Sam dropped his pruning shears and limped towards Heather. She sat up, about to bolt if the old gardener made any threatening gestures, but she couldn't seem to move any further.

Suddenly, the man's demeanor softened and he let out a little grunt as he labored to squat next to the chaise. "Look, little missy, I'm just say'n that young folk like ye and Master Mathew shouldn't be go'n off in areas ye don't know anyth'n 'bout."

Heather stared, holding back a tear. *I'm not the one who violated the house by going through the passageway—it was Matt—he made me,* she was about to say, but stopped herself when she thought better of it. Changing her tactic, she laid her book in her lap and folded her arms across her chest. "I'm sure I don't know what you're referring to."

"Look, little missy. It won't do no good deny'n it. Ye and Master Mathew have been mak'n visits through the magic passage. I know. How do ye think *I* got here? Now, I know ye ain't told no one 'ause ye know no one'd believe ye. I'm not threat'n ye or anyth'n, I'm jus' say'n it ain't proper to go in places ye don't belong and it ain't safe neither.

"Now, I been watch'n ye kiddies since ye first came here, and ye both are nice'ns. I like ye an' I don't want'cha gett'n in any trouble's all."

Heather unfolded her arms. It was no use pretending any longer. And, anyway, she wanted someone else to talk to about it besides Matt. "Oh, Mr. Sam, I'm afraid we've gotten into a terrible mess. But it's not just the passageway it's, it's The Crypt—it's Roger, the butler."

"He's been try'n to go through the magic passage!?"

"Oh, no, Mr. Sam. It's not anything like that. Matt thought he saw Roger rummaging through Aunt Estelle's bedroom while she was in Europe. And Matt thinks he's up to something awful. I think he probably is too because we found out that he used to work for our parents at their company as head of security. So, it's too coincidental to have worked there and now be employed as the butler and chauffer *and* be married to our governess." And without any further thought as to propriety, Heather threw herself into the unsuspecting arms of Sam the gardener.

Sam hadn't ever had a child in his arms before, either as Sam the gardener, or as Thomas Smyth, the old mariner.

"There, there, little one. It'll be right soon enough. Naw, I never liked that Hill fella neither. Not from the first day to this. But what's travel'n through the magic passage have to do with 'im?"

"Well, I'm not sure I know. But I think Matt is planning on visiting a time when our parents were alive and asking them about The Crypt Keeper, I—I mean Roger."

"The Crypt Keeper! Ha, ha, ha. That's a good'n. The Crypt Keeper. Couldn't 'ave picked a better name for 'im meself. Ha.

"Yer both probably right 'bout 'im. I wouldn't put noth'n past 'im. 'E's devious, that one—ye can tell by 'is eyes."

"I just hope Matt can make our parents understand what's happened *and* make them believe he's visiting from the future. Maybe they'll be able to figure out what Roger is up to.

"Matt didn't tell me, but he went through the secret passageway this morning and I just know he's visiting our parents right now. He didn't want me to go with him because I made such a fuss the last time. But it was hard seeing Mommy and Daddy and not be able to hug them or even talk to them."

"Ye mean Master Mathew 'as gone through again? 'Ow many times 'ave ye both been through?"

"I don't know—about ten or twelve, I guess."

"And 'ow long 'ave ye stayed each time?"

"Well, we've mostly stayed close to home for maybe about an hour or so. But, when we visited our old house in Burlingame, to see our parents, it took a while to get there, so we were gone about two hours I guess. Why?"

"Because ye can't stay in another time for more'n four hours—"

"Or you'll be stuck." Heather found herself saying the words in unison with Sam. "So that's what the rest of the riddle is about. *Never tarry longer than when the next watch is struck, or wherever you are you're sure to be stuck.*"

"'At's right, little miss. 'At's why I've come to warn ye both 'bout the magic passage."

And Sam the gardener drifted off into memories of when he was Captain Thomas Smyth, and of how he had the house built.

"In them days, I was a greedy ol' fool. I cheated folks out'a money and built up a tidy little sum for meself. So when me sail'n days was over, I decided to 'ave this 'ere 'ouse built. I 'ad Chinamen work'n for me, an' one of 'em was a magician or someth'n, but 'e said if I was to let 'im go, 'e'd place some magic in my 'ouse that'd make me live past me normal time. So, acourse I said yes. Well, 'e never told me what 'e really meant till the house's completed. Then 'e shows me the magic passage an' 'is tinker'n with me mariner's clock, an' that's when I realized live'n past me normal time simply meant travel'n in time. 'Course by the time I realized what it all meant, I had fulfilled my promise and let 'im go."

Sam the gardener knelt there with a faraway look in his eyes and let out a long sigh. "I had that riddle rit so's I could carve it right next to me clock to remind meself—mostly of 'ow much a fool I was. I been far into the future, an' didn't like it. I been back to the past too, but that didn' do much good, jus' made me melancholy for me sail'n days. Which acourse I could'n do 'cause bein' on a ship'd take more'n four 'ours. So, 'ere I am, spend'n me days in the ol' 'ouse, either in me time as a retired seaman, or here as yer aunt's gardener. Ol' fool."

Compassion welled up in Heather when she saw the tear glistening in Sam's eye. He wasn't as threatening now as he had seemed just moments ago. He was just an old man who was mournful of his past mistakes.

"Achem." Sam cleared his throat and wiped his eyes with his sleeve, grunting as he strained to stand. "Well, at least I 'ave this ol' 'ouse to enjoy. I like carin' for the garden. I was real 'appy ta see yer aunt an' uncle move in. 'E loved this ol' 'ouse as much as me. Sad when 'e died," Sam finished with a sigh, as though losing an old shipmate.

"Ther're more things ye need ta know 'bout the magic passage than jus' not stayin' more'n four 'ours. Jus' 'cause ye can time travel don't give ye the ability ta change nothin', ye understand? If ye try'n mess with what was it'd be disastrous. Leastways that's what I'm a thinkin'. Ye understand me?"

"Yes, I understand. You can visit but you can't change what was," Heather answered, as if speaking to one of her school teachers.

"Oh my gosh! What time is it?" Heather asked abruptly, bringing Sam out of his reverie.

Sam looked at the afternoon sky. "I'd say it's 'bout 'leven and a half 'ours by the clock."

"Matt's been gone almost two and a half hours, and Manar will be calling us for lunch soon. Thank goodness Aunt Estelle will probably be gone all afternoon, so we don't have to worry about her or The Crypt Keeper." Heather quickly picked up her things. "I'm going into the library to make sure no one sees Matt returning. I just hope he's on his way."

"I'll go with ye, missy, best be gettin' back meself." And the two of them hurried as fast as Sam's artificial leg could take him into the house.

As they entered the library, the Saint Michael's clock struck 11:30 a.m., just as Sam had guessed. Heather wasted no time going behind the sofa to the secret passageway. She poked her head through, but there was no sign of Matt. She scooted out, back to the main area of the room.

"I need to be gettin' back soon er it'll be too late fer me," Sam had no sooner finished his sentence when he and Heather heard shuffling behind the sofa.

"Oh Matt, thank goodness you're back. It's almost lunchtime," Heather said exasperated.

Matt straightened his clothes and looked up, stunned to see Sam the gardener standing right next to Heather. Words escaped him.

"Best I leave now, before anyone else comes in," Sam said, grunting again as he knelt on the floor behind the sofa, crawling to the secret opening. His muffled voice was just barely audible. "Don' know 'ow much longer I can be doin' this."

Next was the now familiar sound of the mariner's clock being adjusted, followed by the passageway door being closed.

Matt stood there looking at Heather with a quizzical stare.

"He knows, Matt," Heather said, answering Matt's silent question. "Sam *is* the old captain. And, I know what the rest of the riddle means," she added, matter-of-factly. "You can't stay anywhere in another time for more that four hours or you'll be stuck there forever!"

Chapter 24

It had been almost four weeks since Roger's last visit to Abdula Robdala's house in Kentfield. But the scene played over and over again in his mind and the words echoed in his brain. *"And what if you come up empty-handed, Mr. Hill? What am I to do then?"*

Roger was desperate. He still hadn't found what he was looking for even though he had searched every square inch of the house—including the garage and potting shed.

Unbeknown to him or anyone else, Matt and Heather had taken the SafGen ledgers from the garage shelf and hid them in a box in Matt's closet. They had planned to go through the ledgers without being disturbed, hoping they could find something that would help unravel The Crypt Keeper's mysterious actions.

Roger had feigned off his weekly meetings with Rashi, explaining that he needed the extra time to put everything in order for the presentation to his boss.

"Caliph," Rashi said. "Mr. Hill has cancelled our weekly meetings. He is claiming he needs the time to put everything together for your next visit with him."

Abdula Robdala abruptly stood up, his robe billowing out like a superhero's cape in mid-flight. "I think it is time to pay Mr. Hill a visit. You have followed him, have you not?"

"Oh yes, Caliph. I can show you exactly where he lives."

Chapter 25

It was the weekend again. Aunt Estelle had been invited to go shopping at Neiman Marcus with two of her woman's club friends. The ladies would be staying to have a late lunch at the store's exclusive Rotunda Dining Room, with its 180-degree view of the city. Roger's services wouldn't be needed since one of the ladies would be arriving in her limo to pick Estelle Furgeson up.

Fortunately, Matt and Heather had gone to their rooms to complete their homework Friday night, with the idea of using homework as an excuse to stay in the library most of Saturday morning.

After their aunt's departure, Matt and Heather headed for the library. Once there, Heather explained everything that Sam the gardener had told her about time traveling and not trying to change anything that happened in the past. When she had finished, Matt told her about his private meeting with their father and how he had finally convinced their dad of the truth. "Heather, I've got to go back and see if Dad's found out anything about The Crypt Keeper. But, I need you to stay here again. OK?"

"Yes, it's OK, as long as you promise me we can go see Mommy and Daddy when we can have a pleasant visit with them."

"I promise." And Matt was gone through the passageway again. Matt had set the date on the mariner's clock to Wednesday, October 16th, the evening his dad had told him was the parent/teacher's meeting at school. Matt didn't know it was the same evening of the day Jon Townsend had discovered his trusted head of security bending over his desk, taking covert photographs.

When Matt arrived at his old house, there was a solitary light dimly glowing through the drawn curtains of the living room window. Matt rang the door bell. To his surprise the door quickly opened, as though his father had been standing by, waiting. Jon Townsend grabbed his son's arm, looking around, his eyes flitting from bushes to street to neighbor's front yards, as if he were expecting to see a spy lurking somewhere.

"Come in, son. I've got some startling news. It certainly came as a shock to me anyway," he said to himself. "I caught Roger red-handed today going through our papers and taking photos. I demanded he leave immediately and I took his camera as evidence. I also told him I would be contacting the police." Then under his breath Jon Townsend added, "And to think we trusted that man."

"So that's why he's been rummaging through everything—he's trying to find your research papers in Aunt Estelle's house," Matt said.

"Yes, I'm sure that's what he's doing. But why is he searching there? And, you haven't told me yet why you and Heather are living with your Great-Aunt Estelle."

Matt wasn't sure how to broach the subject with his dad. He had avoided the awful truth before, but he knew he couldn't stall any longer. There was no other way than to tell his dad of the dire circumstances that were to befall his parents.

"Dad, you've accepted that I'm your son visiting you from the future. But, what I'm about to tell you is going to be just as shocking and even more disturbing. And, once you know it, there will be nothing you can do about it." Matt took a long moment for several deep breaths, hoping to shore up his resolve to lay out everything before his father.

Jon Townsend sat on the edge of the ottoman, peering into his son's eyes, eager to hear his tale, but not sure if he was completely prepared to receive the full brunt of whatever it was.

"Dad—there's going to be a terrible earthquake. There will be lots of destruction and lots of people will be injured, some even killed. Dad, you and Mom—"

Jon Townsend interrupted his son. In an instant he knew what would happen. It was as though he had known all along. In fact, as he thought about it, he realized he had had a foreboding feeling for about a week; and finding Roger Hill in his office only intensified the sensation.

"Don't, son. You needn't say anything more."

"Oh, Dad. I wish there were something I could do. Heather and I miss you and Mom so much." Matt flung himself in his dad's arms, holding him tightly as though that might change everything.

Chapter 26

Matt crawled from behind the sofa and slumped into the leather chair opposite it where Heather lay, reading. "Did Daddy have any new information about The Crypt Keeper?" Heather asked, still reading her book.

Matt didn't answer.

"Matt?" Heather said, laying her book in her lap now to look at him.

Matt's eyes were red and slightly swollen. He had obviously been crying. If that weren't telling enough, his posture was a dead giveaway that he was upset. He looked as though he had been defeated in a long, strenuous battle.

"Matt, what's wrong? Didn't Daddy have any information?"

"Huh? Oh, yeah. The Crypt Keeper's looking for Mom and Dad's research papers. Evidently they *had* been successful at discovering how to make smart babies. The Crypt Keeper probably thinks they're hidden here somewhere."

"But why is that making you so sad? You look awful!"

"Because I just told Dad about the earthquake, and that he and Mom are—"

"Oh," Heather said, knowingly. They both sat in silence. Heather was still holding her book but it no longer interested her. Finally she broke the thick silence and asked, "Didn't

Daddy have *any* advice as to how to deal with The Crypt
Keeper?"

"No, after I told him about the earthquake we just held one
another. I didn't feel like talking about anything else. And
then I had to leave."

"But we have no one else to turn to, Matt. And I think we
need to stop The Crypt Keeper. Who knows what it'll all lead
to if he *does* ever find the papers?"

"Don't you think I know that? But what do you want me
to do? It was difficult enough just seeing Dad that way. And
frankly, right now I don't care if the whole world blows up!"

"I know. It would've upset me too to have to tell Dad the
news. I'm sorry you were alone and I couldn't help." Then
after a short pause she added, "What about talking with Sam?
He's the only other person we can trust right now. He knows
about the secret passage and he doesn't like the Crypt Keeper
any more than we do."

"I don't care. You can talk to him if you want to."

"Come with me, Matt. I think Sam's out in the garden
now." And she stood up, laying her book on the sofa to pull
Matt out of his chair.

As they walked out to the garden Heather called to Sam.
Neither noticed Roger in the butler's pantry nearby. He had
been replacing the silver he had just polished, using the time
to try and solve his dilemma at not finding the papers and
trying to devise how he might stall for more time with Abdula
Robdala. Roger was about to step from the pantry into the
kitchen when Heather called out. Instead, he quickly slipped
back to the shadows of the pantry to stealthily spy on the three
of them. But he couldn't hear. He needed to get closer. He
moved to the broom closet near the window. Fortunately, the
window was open and he was thin enough to hide behind the
open broom-closet door and listen. He caught them in the
middle of their conversation.

"But do you think going through the passageway will
help?" Heather was asking Sam.

"I don' think ye 'ave any other choice. I normally wouldn' advise ye te go through, but I think ye should this time."

The three voices grew faint—Sam had ushered Matt and Heather toward the potting shed. It was safer there, and out of hearing range from the house.

No matter. Roger Hill had all the information he needed.

So, there's a passageway, a hidden door, he thought, *probably incorporated somewhere in the house's architecture, but where? What would be the most likely place? The master bedroom? Yeah, that would make sense.* He'd have to get an opportunity to check the room again. *But wait, the library would be another perfect choice. The paneling could easily hide a secret opening.*

It all made perfect sense. No wonder he couldn't find the papers or a key; he was looking in all the wrong places. *I'll bet there's all sorts of treasure hidden in storage behind that secret door.* After all, Mister and Misses Furgeson had tons of all the stuff money could buy. Roger Hill's breathing quickened as his excitement grew at the thought of finding the bounty. He hadn't yet moved from his hiding spot.

And, that old captain, he probably left all sorts of treasures when the house was his. A broad smile brightened Roger Hill's otherwise sullen expression as he thought of all the money he would get from the sale of the research papers, not to mention all the other riches that would soon be his. *Robdala doesn't have to know about the other stuff—that's mine!*

Roger walked from his hiding spot towards the library. His mind was still in full gear. *But why hadn't Madam confided in me about the door's existence?* Roger Hill's devious nature was reflected in his feelings regarding other people. *Just goes to show, you can't rely on anyone's loyalty. I thought I had her complete confidence—guess not!*

But why does Sam know about the passage? Could Madam have confided in him, a lowly gardener? Or, maybe he found it on his own. "I *have* seen him in here, more than he should be for a gardener," Roger said under his breath. He was standing in the middle of the library now, perusing every feature, looking for some tell-tale sign of a hidden door. He began pushing panels. He felt around the edges of the fireplace, hoping to find a secret button.

As he was searching, thoughts began to flood his mind again. *Ah, so that's why those brats spend so much time in the library.* "They go through the hidden door to play with all the stuff. You'd think Madam would have more sense than to let children play with priceless objects!" Roger was already taking ownership of the imaginary riches. Now all he had to do was time the pilfering of the papers and exchange them for the agreed-upon sale price. He was sure no one would notice they were missing. Then he'd go back through the passageway with a bag, and collect as many of the most precious items stored there he could carry and make his getaway. He'd go to the Cayman Islands to spend the rest of his life in luxury. He'd get a really beautiful, young wife this time. Or, maybe he wouldn't limit himself to just one wife, maybe he'd have lots of young girlfriends instead. *Ah, that's going to be the life.*

Even though his thoughts gave him pleasure, not finding the secret passage was beginning to frustrate him. Just as he was about to yell out a profanity, Matt and Heather walked in. Not expecting to find The Crypt Keeper in the room, they both froze on the spot. "Ah, children," The Crypt Keeper said in a mild tone, feigning fondness for them. "Come in, I know this is your favorite room. I was just straightening some of the books. So, what interests you both so much that you spend so many of your hours in here? I'm sure you've had time to read all the books through, at least two or three times."

"We just like it because it's peaceful and quiet," Heather said, not trusting him for a moment.

"But your rooms are peaceful and quiet, *and*, very private. One would think you'd rather be up there. No, I think there's something more that you're not telling me," he added, this time with more severity in his voice.

Neither of them responded. They just stood there, exchanging glares with him.

The Crypt Keeper slowly moved toward them, a menacing grin now beaming across his face. He grabbed both their arms. "I think it's time we had a serious chat. You see, I know what you've both been up to and you *are* going to tell me where the hidden door is!"

Chapter 27

Heather and Matt gave one another quizzical stares. How could The Crypt Keeper know about the secret passage? Had he seen one or both of them go through? If so, why would he be asking where the entrance was and why had he waited 'til now to confront them?

They both tried to wiggle free from The Crypt Keeper's powerful grip. It was beginning to hurt. The Crypt Keeper threw them down on the sofa and loomed over them, placing his hands on their shoulders this time so they couldn't escape. "Now tell me where the hidden door is," he demanded.

"We don't know what you're talking about," Matt said defiantly.

The Crypt Keeper lifted his hand from Matt's shoulder and slapped him squarely across the face.

"Stop that, you bully," Heather screamed. "You don't deserve to know anything."

"You *will* tell me," The Crypt Keeper answered emphatically and grabbed Heather's arm, twisting it back in an awkward angle, causing her excruciating pain. The Crypt Keeper's foul breath felt hot on Heather's face as he bent down over her, his yellow eyes glowing with rage.

The sound of the door bell startled him and he stood up quickly, releasing her. She was crying now and rubbing her aching arm. Matt put his arms around her to comforter her.

"Who in the blazes could that be?" Roger said. As butler, it was his duty to answer whoever was at the door. "I'll be back. You stay right there. We're not through yet!"

As Roger approached the front doors, he could see two familiar figures through the leaded glass. But there was a third, larger man Roger hadn't seen before. "How did they find *this* place?" he said to himself.

"Mr. Robdala, Rashi, uh, and I'm sorry?" he said, staring blankly at the large stranger. No name was offered. "Come in, come in. I'm flattered that you took the time to visit me, but you needn't have. Everything is working out fine." Roger Hill's demeanor had drastically changed from just a few moments ago. His voice was apologetic and he kept clasping his hands and bowing as he walked backwards, toward the library.

"So, you lead me to believe that you have finally found what you promised to deliver, Mr. Hill," Robdala said, in a not very reassuring tone.

"Well, achem, I don't actually have it yet." Roger held up his hands to waive off the threatening advance the large, nameless man was making on him.

Abdula Robdala raised a single hand and the large man stopped. "And?" Robdala said.

"You see, the reason I couldn't find anything in the past was because there's a storage room behind a hidden door. Madam never confided in me as to its whereabouts. So, naturally I—"

"And you now know where it is, Mr. Hill?" Robdala interrupted.

"Well, no." The large man advanced again. "But, I know who *does* know. And I was just getting that information when you rang." Roger was speaking in short, quick bursts.

They were finally in the library. Matt and Heather hadn't moved. The sound of visitors lulled them into thinking they had a reprieve from The Crypt Keeper's interrogation.

"So whom were you expecting to get the information from, Mr. Hill?" Robdala asked.

Roger pointed towards the sofa where Matt and Heather were seated, about to explain.

"Those two? But they are mere children."

"But they know," insisted The Crypt Keeper, in an almost pleading voice.

"And what are your names?" Robdala said, ignoring Roger Hill and focusing completely on Matt and Heather now. He sat in the chair, adjusting his robes.

"I'm Master Mathew Townsend and this is my sister, Miss Heather Townsend," Matt said with dignity and pride.

"Well, I am honored to meet you both. It's a pleasure to know such intelligent, mannerly children. In this day and age I didn't think such was possible."

Matt gave a quizzical glance at Rashi and the large man.

"Oh, excuse my manners, young Master Mathew. These are my associates. May I present Rashi? Rashi, Master Mathew and Miss Heather Townsend."

Rashi smiled broadly and rushed to shake their hands. "That will be all, Rashi—a simple 'How do you do' will suffice. We needn't be that formal." Rashi stepped back.

"And this is my bodyguard, Ali." Ali bowed. The long, curved sword at his side stuck out at an obtrusive ninety-degree angle to his body. It hadn't been so obvious just a minute ago, but now it caused Heather to inhale in an audible gasp.

"I understand you both have some important information that would make this assemblage quite happy," Robdala said in a low, calm voice in an attempt to stem their fears and gain their confidence.

"You see, the items we seek will bring fame to your family name, which you may or may not know had been tarnished. With the untimely death of your parents, there was no one or no way to clear it up. But we believe we have found a way."

115

"Our name has not been tarnished!" Heather almost shouted.

Matt placed his hand on her arm to quiet her. "Sir, we were not aware of our name being cast with those of ill repute," Matt said. "And neither I nor my sister appreciates the suggestion of such."

Abdola Robdala straightened upright in his chair. His body stiffened at the hint of defiance this mere child displayed towards him. He had been patient with Roger Hill long enough. He had no more patience left for these children.

"It is pertinent that we gain that information. I am normally a very patient man, young Master Mathew, but I am not willing to wait any longer. I will ask you one more time. If you do not respond favorably, I'm afraid Ali will have to ply his trade. And I assure you, he is very good at what he does!"

Matt stared at Ali with defiance; Heather stared at Ali's saber with fear.

Sam had been in the potting shed storing the gardening tools and cleaning up. When he had finished, he hung up his canvas apron and gloves and walked to the house. It was getting precariously close to his departure time. When he opened the library doors expecting that Roger and the children might be in there, he was surprised instead to see three strange visitors.

"And who is this?" Robdala asked.

"It's Sam, Madam's gardener. He's the other one that knows," Roger said.

"Knows what?" Sam asked. "An' who ar' these exotics?"

"It's none of your business who they are. You exceed your bounds, gardener. I don't know why Madam puts up with you." Roger had regained some of his old bravado and was happy to have someone to wield it on. "You have no right to be in the house. Your place is in the garden. If I had my way you wouldn't be here at all," Roger added with disdain.

"Ali," Robdala said, and gestured for the large man to grab Sam and place him on the sofa next to Matt and Heather.

Ali grabbed Sam's arm and flung him down. Heather looked up at Sam with sympathy. But Sam returned her glance with a smile and a wink, as though everything were going to be all right.

Chapter 28

The commotion downstairs easily awoke Manar. Her nap had been restless. She got up and straightened her bed, and went to her bathroom to quickly comb her hair and brush her teeth. When she felt presentable she went downstairs to see if she might be needed to bring refreshments to the guests.

Manar gently knocked on the library doors. No one responded but she could hear muffled voices—and they didn't sound pleasant. She knocked again, louder this time.

Roger Hill went to the door and opened it only wide enough to speak to Manar through the crack. "What do you want, woman? Can't you see we're doing business in here?"

"I only thought you might want me to bring some refreshments—to your guests?" she added quizzically. *What business would he have and why would he bring guests into the house?* she thought.

"Bring her in, Mr. Hill," Robdala said.

Roger grabbed Manar and pulled her into the room. He needn't pretend any longer, everything was coming to an end, a very favorable end.

"What's going on?" Manar said when she saw Matt, Heather, and Sam on the sofa with a very large man hovering over them in a threatening stance.

Heather looked up at Manar. Her expression wasn't so

much one of fright, but more of sympathy for Manar. As though she were thinking *I'm so sorry you're involved in this now.*

Ali was about to grab Heather when Sam stood up. "It's no use pretending any longer, youngin's. We may as well fess up."

"Well, well. You see, Mr. Hill? This man is very intelligent for a mere gardener. It is quite amazing how the thought of a little pain can suddenly bring enlightenment to a person." And Robdala gave out the sinister laugh of a tyrant over the oppressed.

Sam began walking towards the back of the sofa and Ali drew his saber, thinking Sam was about to try something foolish. "Jus' goin' ta the passage. It *is* in a secret place after all."

"And, where might that be, gardener?" Robdala asked.

"Behind the sofa," Sam answered. No one was the least bit suspicious at how willing Sam was to reveal the secret passageway. One thing was sure, though, Sam was eager to get back through, or it would definitely be all over for him!

Ali looked at Robdala for permission. Robdala nodded. Ali shoved the sofa aside.

There was nothing there. Nothing that was obvious anyway.

"And where is it, gardener?" Robdala demanded. Roger stood by, wringing his hands, his heart pounding and his thoughts once again drifting to the riches.

Sam gave his grunt and knelt down in front of the paneling. He took out his pocket knife and slid it around an almost invisible slot. There was the low click and the door opened.

Roger rushed towards it but Sam put out a hand to stop him. "There's somethin' ye all need ta know 'bout this 'ere passage. Jus' 'cause the door opened doesn' mean ye can go through 'at easily. Ye 'ave ta adjust this 'ere timepiece. It's like a lock on a vault, ye see."

"Ah, very cleaver," Robdala said.

"Now, let me jus' adjust it 'ere," Sam said, while he set the time to May 10, 1916. "Right then. She's ready."

The four men were about to rush the entrance when Sam added, "There's still one more thin'. The room's more like a basement and ye 'ave ta take a ramp to get down there. Jus' be careful when ye go down. Follow me."

The Crypt Keeper rushed towards the passageway, but Robdala stopped him with his hand. "I would be happy to let you go first, Mr. Hill. But we are not leaving without the children and their governess. Ali, take Master Mathew and Miss Heather. Rashi, do you think you can manage the young woman?" Rashi nodded with a delightful grin.

Ali already had Matt and Heather in each arm and was about to go down the ramp. Matt hoped it would hold the three of them.

Rashi shoved Manar to the entrance and grabbed her in an unseemly way from behind. They were both through in tandem.

"Mr. Hill, please," Robdala said, gesturing towards the opening.

They were all assembled in the center of the room, at the base of the ramp. It was strange seeing a ramp extending out from the top of a fireplace into a room. A room, by the way, that seemed to be an exact duplicate of the one they had all just left.

"Very artful," Robdala said. "A storage room made up to look similar to the library upstairs. I must inquire, if ever I get the chance, as to whom Madam hired as the decorator. Very clever.

"Now, enough amusement. Look through the bookshelves. The papers are most likely stored in a book, or perhaps the books conceal a wall safe."

Ali and Rashi *and* The Crypt Keeper rushed to the shelves. They began rummaging through the books, almost tearing out the pages, discarding them in a heap on the floor when nothing was found. The four men were so engrossed in their search they hadn't noticed that Sam had gathered Matt, Heather, and Manar to the opposite corner of the room. Nor had they noticed the sword he was wielding.

"Leave me things be," he demanded.

"What?" the four men said in unison, and wheeled around to see the strangest sight. Sam the gardener, now in his own time dimension, stood there as Captain Thomas Smyth. He had one arm raised high in an arch above his head, the other poised in front of him pointing the sword forward, his stance in a lunge—he was on guard.

Ali began laughing as he pulled his saber from its sheath. "You are no match for Ali," Robdala said. "But I admire your chivalry at trying to protect the weak," he added with a motion toward Matt, Heather, and Manar.

"Try me," the old captain said, knowing that he could not be pierced by someone from another time.

Robdala gestured in the direction of the old captain. Ali understood. Holding the saber in both hands, he swung it in a half circle high above his own head. In one continuous motion he lunged toward the captain, completing the full circle of the swing. If the blow had engaged, it would have split the captain in two, down the middle.

Ali stood there dazed. His saber had seemingly sliced straight through the old man like butter, the tip striking the floor with a loud thud. But Sam was unscathed. Ali looked like a statue with his saber straight in front of him with only the tip touching the floor between Sam's outstretched legs. *Could the old man be that agile as to step aside missing the blow and return to his original position at such lightning speed that no one could actually see his movements?*

Everyone else stood frozen too. Even though Matt and Heather knew they were all mere holograms to the captain, they had momentarily forgotten it in the heat of the action.

But he was also a hologram to them and really couldn't hurt any of them either. How was he going to deal with the situation?

In spite of his peg leg, the captain was quite agile. He gave out a laugh and, still holding out his own sword, he moved backward until he was standing just in front of the children and Manar. "Run now. Ye know what ye mus' do."

Matt and Heather grabbed Manar's hands and left through the library's double doors towards the entry.

"After them, Mr. Hill. Rashi, go with him," Robdala said. "Ali and I can handle this one." And Robdala drew his small pearl-handled dagger.

Matt and Heather's youth allowed them to run quickly. Fortunately, Manar's adrenalin levels had shot up, giving her the ability to keep up. But Rashi and Roger Hill were close on their heels.

Matt spotted a horse-drawn ice wagon on the corner that was about to pull away from the curb. "Hurry," he said, and grabbed Heather's hand again. The three ran down the sidewalk, one behind the other like a human chain. "Jump on the back," Matt said. The ice man had left the wagon's tailgate down for convenience, since he had so many frequent stops to make. Matt was the first to get on. Heather was close behind and Matt reached down just in time to help her on when the ice man cracked his whip and urged his horse to move. Manar was struggling to catch up. Both the children knelt on the edge of the tailgate reaching to grab Manar. Matt made contact and pulled. Heather grabbed Manar by the arm and pulled too. Finally, Manar was aboard.

None of them minded sitting in the melting ice water that had collected on the tailgate. But Manar's head was swirling with confusion. This hadn't been a good day. She had awakened with a raging headache, and her attempt at a nap hadn't helped alleviate it. Now she was running from her own husband and three strange Middle Eastern men whom she had never met before, *and* in the strangest of surroundings.

Roger Hill and Rashi had almost caught up with the three of them as the ice wagon pulled safely away. Roger wasn't going to give up that easily though. He spotted another horse-drawn wagon just about to leave the curb too, but he wasn't about to rely on the driver. He jumped aboard, shoving the milkman from his seat as he grabbed the reins. Rashi swerved to miss the falling milkman and jumped on just in time, sliding on the seat beside Roger as the wagon jerked forward.

Roger Hill was so intent on the situation, he hadn't had time to think about how strange the surroundings were. But they certainly caught Rashi's attention. "Ice wagons and milkmen?" he said. "I thought this was an advanced country."

"They're probably making a movie. They do that a lot in the city," Roger said, whipping the horse to go faster.

Manar hadn't questioned anything. She just wanted to reach safety. The whole situation had brought up ugly childhood memories of her and her mother and brother trying to flee Iran.

Chapter 29

The ice wagon meandered through the neighborhood. But, in spite of leaving well ahead, the three soggy passengers on the tailgate could see the milk wagon's frenzied horse making its rapid advance on them due to Roger's incessant whipping. Because he was more interested in speed than in how to rein in the horse, and because he really wasn't a horseman, the wagon was swerving wildly from side to side, almost causing Roger and Rashi to fly out the open doorways.

The ice wagon, by contrast, was making its steady progression around the corner to the next block when at the far end of Marina Boulevard came a team of horses pulling a fire wagon, bell clanging to alert motorists, buggies, and pedestrians alike.

Either Roger didn't notice or didn't care. He continued on, whipping non-stop. But it was more than the milk wagon's steed could bear. Its nostrils flared and its eyes opened wide in wild panic. It was already agitated by its novice driver when the milk and fire wagons reached the corner at the same time. Rashi screamed a warning, diverting Roger's attention from the wagon he was pursuing. The oncoming team was so close Roger could see vapor rising from the four steaming horses, their manes wet and muscles bulging. It was too late.

The fireman pulled on his reins, hoping to avoid the unavoidable. His horses obeyed and swerved, missing the lone milk-wagon horse. But the angle of the milk wagon itself, as it approached the corner, placed it in just the right position to be hit by the side of the fire wagon.

Fortunately, Matt, Heather, and Manar were at a safe enough distance to avoid being part of the impending calamity; and fortunately Matt had the presence of mind to get them off their own wagon just seconds before the collision taking place half a block away. The three of them stood on the sidewalk and watched the scene as it unfolded before them.

The impact severed the milk wagon's harnessing, allowing the panicked horse to run wildly free, dragging what remained of the rigging in the roadway. The wagon teetered sideways and finally fell, crashing and sliding into a wrought-iron fence surrounding a stately house on the corner.

Roger and Rashi were also able to jump just seconds before the wagon they were on crashed. They lay in a heap, dazed and disheveled.

Matt didn't want to allow the two men enough time to get their bearings. He grabbed Heather by the hand and yelled, "Come on, let's get out of here!"

"Where to?" Heather yelled back as she followed Matt, who had begun running west.

"I don't know. But remember what Sam told us? We gotta try and keep them out of our time dimension." Matt panted, breathless from running and talking at the same time.

Heather knew Matt was right. This had been their plan all along, but they hadn't counted on having to contend with three foreigners too. She just hoped Sam, in his familiar role as Captain Thomas Smyth, would be able to handle Abdola Robdala and Ali.

The ice wagon's route had taken the three to Scott Street. After the collision, Matt had begun heading west again on Jefferson. Their proximity to Sam's row house gave Matt an idea. He turned north on Divisadero. "We're going in circles, Matt. What are you doing?"

"We're going back to the house."

"Back to the house? Do you think that's a good idea?"

"Yeah. Trust me." Matt didn't want to get entangled with the crowd that had begun gathering down the block to watch the fire brigade put out the small grass fire at the entrance to the Presidio.

In minutes, they were at the side gate to the house's back yard. Matt pulled on the chain. The latch disengaged and the gate swung open. He motioned for Heather and Manar to go through to the garden. "Head for the kitchen and into the library, quick."

As they ran past the potting shed, a surprising but welcomed sight caught their eyes. Sam and a member of his household staff, who had served under him aboard ship, had Robdala and Ali in wrist and ankle irons. The shackles were so huge that Robdala and Ali were convinced there was no escape for them, and so they sat, subdued. Had they known the large hammered restraints were mere holograms to them it would have put a damper on Sam's and the children's plans.

Just as Matt, Heather, and Manar were about to enter the kitchen, they heard Roger and Rashi stumble through the gate into the yard.

Roger's rage was at such a fever pitch his first intent was to catch Matt and Heather for the sheer pleasure of slapping, then restraining them. Once his revenge was satisfied, he'd force them into telling him where the papers might be stored in the mock library/storage room.

Rashi, on the other hand, was only obeying orders and blindly followed Roger in pursuit of the children. Neither noticed Robdula and Ali in the shed.

The three entered the library. Heather noticed that the ramp they had used for their original entry into the library was no longer extending out from atop the fireplace. Matt quickly headed for the back of the settee. "Are we going back to our house?" Heather asked.

"No. I've got a better idea." Matt set the clock to 8:45 a.m., Thursday, October 17, 1989, pausing long enough for Roger and Rashi to see them behind the settee.

They were through the passageway and headed down the ramp, first Heather, then Manar, and lastly Matt. Matt wanted to stick his tongue out at Roger in mocking defiance to incite The Crypt Keeper to follow, but decided that wasn't the mature thing to do.

Roger caught sight of Matt and headed for the settee. So intent on his pursuit he hadn't realized he was not ascending a ramp to the library where the trip had begun—but was about to slide down still another ramp to still another library.

Matt threw caution to the wind. He wasn't as careful this time about not alarming the household staff of intruders as he had been the previous times he had entered. He just hoped his timing was right.

Heather and Manar followed Matt, Heather trying to guess what plan Matt had devised; Manar just running for her life with the only two people in the world she dared trust.

The bus pulled up just as they approached the stop. The three boarded. Matt dropped in the fare and headed for the rear seats.

Roger and Rashi reached the bus just as the driver closed the doors. Roger pounded on the door and the driver motioned for him to clear the doorway as he pushed the lever. The mechanism let out a gush of air, and the doors opened. Roger and Rashi ascended the steps and Roger eyed the passengers as he shuffled in his pockets for the correct change, upset that he had to pay Rashi's fare too.

The bus was crowded. Roger spotted the three fugitives and found a single seat facing them. Rashi had to stand. Roger glared at Matt through his bushy eyebrow, agitated that his prey was so close but that he was unable to do anything about it without causing the wrath of the other passengers to come down on him for "abusing women and children."

The three sat silently too, watching their assailant. The bus finally reached Fourth and King Streets. Matt gestured for Heather and Manar to exit the rear bus doors and head for the ticket booth. Roger was taken by surprise at their quick descent and he and Rashi got tangled in the crowd of passengers leaving and entering the bus.

"Three please, two children and one adult," Matt told the ticket teller.

"You're just in time, young man. The train's about to depart."

Matt gently pushed Manar and Heather onto the steep step of the train then pulled himself up with the assistance of the handrail mounted at the side of the doorway. *Come on*, he thought. *Don't be so slow. Get your tickets and get on.* He was silently talking to The Crypt Keeper.

Matt found an empty row of seats for the three of them. It was facing the doorway. *Where are they?*

Yes! Finally, Matt said to himself as he saw Roger and Rashi entering the car. They were out of breath and stumbled into a row of passengers as the train abruptly pulled away from the station.

There were only two aisle seats available about three rows away from Matt, Heather and Manar. The two thugs sat down, Roger resuming his glare.

Ordinarily, a trip on the train would have been a pleasant ride, with the rocking motion each car made as it sped along the interlocking tracks, clickity-clicking in hypnotic rhythm. But the situation was so intense the three fugitives sat upright, their bodies tensed for instant reaction.

It was a long thirty minuets to the Milbrea station, and as the train slowed to a stop, passengers who wanted to disembark had already begun queuing near the exits. Roger took advantage of the opportunity to grab an open seat just opposite the three before new passengers boarded.

After five minuets the train again jerked forward. The

sudden movement caused Roger to be thrown right into Manar's lap. Being that close to her and the children added fresh fuel to his rage, and finally got the better of him. He grabbed Manar and Matt's arms, trapping Heather in the middle.

"You think you're clever don't you, little man?" Roger said, looking at Matt. "What do you think of your precious darlings now, you stupid woman?" he added without looking at Manar. "Look what they've dragged you into." Manar couldn't look into Roger's eyes. *How could I have been so stupid? I thought you loved me, but now I see you never did.*

Heather tried to slide down the front of her seat and out between The Crypt Keeper's legs. She wasn't sure what she would do if she got free. Having him hovering over her that way was causing her to feel claustrophobic. But, before she could manage a successful escape, Roger raised his knee and shoved her back down. "You're not going anywhere," he said, his voice getting louder.

Matt could see that their stop was fast approaching. If his plan were to work, they had to get off. He noticed that a few passengers had glanced in their direction at the sound of Roger's raised voice, but quickly turned away, not wanting to get involved.

Matt had a flash of genius. "No, Dad, you can't take us away from Mom. We won't go with you," he suddenly shouted and bent over and bit Roger's hand.

Immediately, Roger released both he and Manar, grabbing his own throbbing hand instead. This time, the commotion caused nearby passengers to stare in their direction.

Matt took advantage of the situation. "We're not going back to live with you. We won't take those beatings anymore!" Matt shouted, playing his role to the hilt, all the while motioning for Heather and Manar to get up and move closer to the exit.

Roger stood there for a moment, dumbfounded. He hadn't expected this outburst from Matt.

The train had come to a stop at the Burlingame station and the doors opened. Matt gently pushed Heather and Manar to the steps, following close behind. Roger rushed towards them, but a young male passenger grabbed his shoulder. "You're not going anywhere, mister. I know what it's like to be abused by a parent."

"Yeah," someone else said. "There are laws against child abuse ya know."

Roger gave the young man a look of disdain. He pulled the man's hand off his shoulder and pushed him against exiting passengers, knocking everyone aside.

"Has the whole world gone crazy?" he said as he rushed to the line of awaiting taxis.

Rashi was on his own. As a swarm of new passengers boarded, he had been pushed back into a seat. He tried explaining that he wanted off, but the more nervous he got the harder it was for him to recall his English. The two other passengers in his row finally understood and folded their legs close to the seat so Rashi could squeeze past. Now all he had to do was make it through the crowded car. There was hardly any standing room left and he pushed and shoved his way to the exit. Unfortunately, as he got there the train again jerked forward, continuing its trip southward. He was stuck on a foreign train in a foreign country, without his caliph. Rashi was justifiably frightened. *Where was he headed? How would he get back? Would the caliph wait for him?*

Chapter 30

Roger Hill quickly entered the next taxi in line. "Follow that cab!" he shouted at the driver. "Don't lose them!"

Roger was leaning on the back of the driver's seat, peering over his shoulder, when it suddenly dawned on him that this was familiar territory. He hadn't been here in ages, but it was unmistakable. *But why are they going here?*

"Mr. Jon Townsend. Please, we have to see him immediately!" Matt forced out the words as he panted for air.

The receptionist stood up startled. Never in her long employment with SafGen had anyone rushed in like this. Even when there had been threats by animal rights protesters who disregarded the company's insistence that no animals were ever used in testing.

"It's all right, Ms. Albright. Matt, what are you doing here? Heather?" Jon had just seen his eleven-year-old daughter for the first time. She was growing to be more beautiful than he'd imagined. Jon smiled at Manar with the greatest appreciation that she was still caring for his children.

Manar's eyes opened in wide-eyed shock at seeing her deceased employer alive again, and speaking to her as casually as he had done so many times before. It was too much for her mind to grasp and she fell onto the lobby sofa in a faint. "Ms. Albright, get Manar some water, please," Jon said.

Heather ran to her father and squeezed him around the legs as she had done so many times as a toddler.

"Dad, we haven't got much time. Roger's—" No sooner had the words left Matt's mouth than Roger Hill pushed through the entrance. He stood there stunned. *What was going on? The company was sold long ago. Why in the heck is someone impersonating Jon Townsend?*

"Mr. Townsend, would you like me to call security?" Ms. Albright asked, knowing Roger Hill had been terminated the day before.

"No, I don't think that will be necessary, Ms. Albright. Thank you." Then Jon Townsand turned to his former head of security and said, "I know what you want. Follow me. I think we can work this out like adults."

Roger was confused, but he followed the Townsend look-alike anyway.

"Don't trust him, Dad," Matt said. "He's gotten other people involved."

"Yeah, they're foreigners and I don't like them, Daddy," Heather added.

"Don't worry. It's all going to be OK." Jon Townsend knew what to do. He remembered everything Matt had told him about time travel.

So, this is where the papers have been hidden, Roger thought to himself. *But I did a thorough search of this area.*

They had gathered in the back of the building near the high-value security cage, leaving Manar in Ms. Albright's care. The company had installed the cage at Roger's insistence. He had learned at a security conference that any company using expensive equipment or supplies should keep everything under lock and key with proper checkout procedures to avoid internal theft.

"After you," Jon said, and Roger fell for the ruse. Quickly, Jon closed the swing gate, locking Roger inside.

Matt knew what his dad was up to. Roger was stuck there. "Dad, we have to go, now."

"I know, son."

"But Daddy, we're going to be back when we can have a nice visit with you and Mommy. We promise."

"I'll be looking forward to it, sweetheart."

Jon Townsend watched his children leave with Manar. He was proud of them and glad he and their mother had selected Manar as their nanny. It had been a good choice.

Somehow, knowing his fate hadn't made Jon Townsend sad. He had, however, debated with himself whether or not to tell Josie, eventually opting not to tell her. In spite of her disciplined scientific thinking, he knew the thought of her not being there for her children would be more than she could bear.

There would be plenty of time to tell her when the children visited again—in the future? in the past? He laughed to himself. *No matter, pardon the pun—it's all simultaneous.*

Guess the quantum physicists had it right all along.

Chapter 31

On the trip back to San Francisco, Matt and Heather explained everything to Manar—about The Crypt Keeper's ploy to get entrance into their aunt's home to look for the research papers, and about time travel, and who Sam the gardener really was.

They finally made it back to the ramp in the 1989 library. Apparently, no one had been in to attend to the room all day. Matt pushed the lever and the ramp flipped over to reveal its steps. "Go ahead, just climb up, Manar," Matt said.

"It's easy. Here, follow me," Heather added.

Matt was the last one up. As he crawled through the passageway to the library in his great-aunt's house, the muffled sound of the clock's disengaged bell struck eight times, announcing the next watch. They had made it back just in time.

Meanwhile, somewhere at the train depot in San Jose, Rashi staggered in a weakened state. Hardly anyone noticed the strange man slowly fading as if made of mist. But a short article on the back page of the next morning's *Chronicle* stated that three people insisted they saw a man completely disappear before their eyes. The article added that it was probably a pre-publicity stunt for the new David Copperfield event at the Cow Palace.

In the potting shed, in the 1916 garden, Sam and his old shipmate watched the two shackled men slowly disappear. " 'At was some powerful magic the ol' Chinaman gave ye, cap'in. Guess those two won't be givin' no one any more trouble."

And, in the back of the 1989 SafGen building, Jon Townsend watched as Roger Hill faded away. "Your greed got the better of you, Roger. I think you're getting what you deserve. Maybe you'll make some better choices wherever you end up."

Manar had been visibly shaken when Estelle Furgeson arrived home late from her day of social activities and so she assumed it was because Roger was nowhere to be found.

Matt, Heather and Manar had agreed not to tell Aunt Estelle of the secret passage, nor of Roger's deceit, nor of the foreign intruders. She probably wouldn't have believed them anyway. And, attracting attention to a secret passage and time travel didn't seem the wise thing to do.

When the authorities arrived to fill out the missing person report, they found both cars still in the garage, and no sign of foul play.

No one reported Abdola Robdala, Rashi, or Ali missing.

Epilogue

Matt was glad Heather had insisted they return home for the holidays. Visiting her and Great-Aunt Estelle during winter break was a welcomed respite from his heavy class schedule at Stanford's School of Humanities and Sciences. Even though he was attending university so close to home, his studies had left him little time to relax or socialize.

As Matt stood in the library, he touched the keys of the old pipe organ still sitting in its spot below the captain's portrait. "One of these days Aunt Estelle will *have* to get this fixed," he said to himself with a chuckle. He strode across the Persian carpet and settled in his uncle's favorite, leather wing-back chair, listening to the crackle of the fire and admiring the richly colored holiday ornaments on the large fir tree.

Thoughts were still flooding his mind. Matt realized how much he admired and loved his Great-Aunt Estelle. In spite of her age, she was still enjoying her role as a socialite. When he had arrived the night before, he had just enough time to shower and get dressed for their evening out. Heather and his aunt were already dressed and waiting when he arrived. His aunt had donned her finest for the Opera's gala winter program, and as he helped her get in the old Lincoln Town Car, she commented at how proud she was to have her handsome young nephew and beautiful niece as escorts.

Matt gave out another chuckle. He would have hated an event like that when he was thirteen. Now, though, he was thankful for having been exposed to the finest cultural events a city such as San Francisco had to offer.

"You look comfortable." Her voice was still sweet and innocent at eighteen as it had been at eleven. Heather entered the library with a tray of hot chocolate. "Manar made this for us. She thought you might enjoy a cup when she remembered how much we liked it as kids."

Moments later, Manar came in with a tray of baked treats. Matt followed her with his eyes. *She never ages. She's still as beautiful now as she was when she first came to us. She'll be a great mother.* Matt was happy Manar had found Javid. He was a handsome, gentle man who was just as excited about becoming a new parent as Manar. "Javid will be joining us soon, he's checking the back door. Madam is all settled in for the evening. I brought her some hot chocolate too."

"So how's your first year at Northwestern going?" Matt asked Heather. "Still want to be a stage designer? Guess Aunt Estelle is thrilled that all that culture she introduced us to rubbed off on one of us."

Heather laughed. "It's wonderful. I love Chicago. Yeah, I still think theater's the life for me. How 'bout you—still want to follow in the folks' footsteps?"

"Yeah. I'd like to carry on with their vision. It's not just a matter of creating intelligence, though, I think it's unlocking that intelligence that's the key. We all have unlimited potential."

"But your real interest is in the whole 'time thing' right?"

"You got me. No matter how many times we've been through that passageway, I can't figure it out."

"Guess that's the difference with us 'artistic types,'" Heather said. "We just enjoy the trip."

The End

Printed in the United States
54450LVS00002B/1-33